THREE FACES OF LOVE is the first English translation of three short novels by Emile Zola, author of NANA and the most outspoken critic of manners and morals in nineteenth century France.

FOR ONE NIGHT OF LOVE tells the deliberately horrifying story of Thérèse de Marsanne, a rich and corrupt aristocrat whose perverse sexual appetites lead her to the gruesome murder of her own lover.

ROUND TRIP, a tender story of a young couple on their honeymoon, is also a vigorous attack on the middle class morality which puts a higher value on money than on love.

MONSIEUR CHABRE: Against the background of the surf pounding the Atlantic coastline, a husband devours winkles to fortify his virility while a handsome stranger pursues—and captures —his willing wife on the sands below.

THREE FACES OF LOVE

EMILE ZOLA

Three Faces of Love

Translated from French
by Roland Grant

SPHERE

SPHERE BOOKS LTD
30/32 Gray's Inn Road, London, W.C.1

This translation © Roland Grant, 1969

First Sphere Books edition, 1969

TRADE MARK

SPHERE

Set in Baskerville 12/14 pt.

Printed in Great Britain
by Richard Clay (The Chaucer Press), Ltd., Bungay, Suffolk

INTRODUCTION

EMILE ZOLA was born on April 2, 1840, in Paris. His father was an engineer of Italian–Greek descent. The family went back to Aix-en-Provence, where the boy was brought up. After his father's death in 1846, poverty and the possessive love of the mother for her only child molded his character and left their marks on him for ever. Emile attended the Lycée St. Louis at Aix —one of his school friends was the future painter Cézanne—and, later, universities in Paris and Marseilles.

In 1860 Zola settled in Paris and worked for six years as a clerk at Hachette's bookshop. Hachette rejected his first volume of stories, which was published by Lacroix in 1864 under the title *Contes à Ninon* (*Tales for Ninon*). Shortly after, Zola acquired French citizenship and began to meet such leading literary figures as Saint-Beuve and Michelet. In 1865 his novel *La confession de Claude* (*Claude's Confession*) was published—and denounced to the Public Prosecutor as a dangerous book. At about that time he married, but his marriage turned out a failure and, in 1888, Zola took as his mistress a laundry maid from Médan, Jeanne Rogerat, who bore him two children.

Zola's first 'realistic' novel was *Thérèse Raquin* (1868), which made a great stir. He then started to map out his twenty-volume ROUGON-MACQUART series, the complex chronicle of two interlinked families living in the late sixties, during the decline of the French Second Empire. As a safely entrenched but always controversial author, he intervened publicly in the infamous Dreyfus Affair, at a critical stage when the innocence of the Jewish officer of the General Staff, wrongly convicted of spying and sent to Devil's Island for life, had become the subject of bitter political controversy. Zola published an open letter, the celebrated *J'Accuse* (*I Accuse*), in which he indicted the War Office for hushing up the truth about the case. He was prosecuted and sentenced to a year's imprisonment but escaped to England and returned to France a popular hero, after Dreyfus's final vindication in 1899.

Zola's last work was the planning of a series he called *The Four Gospels*. Only three were completed and published: *Fruitfulness, Work,* and *Truth*. Justice would have followed, but Zola died suddenly on September 28, 1902, from carbon monoxide poisoning caused by a blocked chimney in his bedroom.

In 1908, his body was transferred to the Pantheon.

When Zola wrote of Balzac, 'What a man! He crushes the whole country with his weight,' his words could have applied equally to himself. His hypersensitivity, his constant preoccupation with smells and sounds and color, made him a poet, while his analytical powers and a deep conviction of the evil that lay at the roots of society supplied both his force and his realism. These combined gifts, and a monumental capacity for ceaseless work, enabled him to achieve his incomparable picture of France and the French of his times.

Zola examined the fabric of nineteenth-century France, tested every strand for strength and color, noted stains and the dirt that had been swept out of sight—and then rewove his own interpretation in the ROUGON-MACQUART series of twenty novels. In this stupendous achievement no aspect of French life escaped his meticulous attention and brilliant powers of characterization and description. The mentality and morals, weaknesses, and ambitions of noble families and bourgeoisie were recorded; the drudgery, poverty, courage, and hopelessness of railway workers, masons, prostitutes, and peasants were set vividly and unforgettably before the eyes of readers who were frequently outraged and infuriated.

Zola's work often aroused anger. There is probably no other author who was the object of such vitriolic hatred and violent criticism in his lifetime. He laid bare the acquisitive, narrow, and conformist souls of the middle classes and incurred their enmity. He pin-pointed the moral weakness and corruption in the army—that led to the disastrous defeat by the Prussians—in *La débâcle*, which was compared to Tolstoy's *War and Peace* and earned Zola the loathing of St. Cyr and everything it stood for. He went further, and exposed in *J'Accuse* the virulent anti-Semitism that existed in the army. He attacked the Roman Catholic Church in *La faute de l'abbé Mouret* and in *Lourdes* and *Rome*, and attracted the fury of *les gens bien-pensants*. And in *Nana*, in particular, he shocked the innocent and embarrassed the guilty by his picture of the degradation that lust could bring, the corruption and disease that attended sexual promiscuity. And, by equating the once-beautiful, rotting body of Nana the prostitute with the body politic of France, as Nana lay dying and the crowds in the streets screamed 'To Berlin,' he struck simultaneously at private sexuality and national pride.

Where do the three stories especially translated into English for this volume, fit into the pattern of Zola's work, both as chronicler of his times and moral reformer? What have the three stories in common? Were they three facets of life as lived in nineteenth-century France, three aspects of sexuality, or three tracts written to illustrate selected themes? Were they written at widely-spaced intervals? And what relation do they bear to Zola's life and the mainstream of his work at the time they were written?

A few years ago, while engaged in research on another project, I reread *Pot-Bouille* in order to get the atmosphere of the transformation Paris underwent just over a century ago. Narrow, winding streets were being torn down and the wide, straight avenues and boulevards planned by Haussman and familiar to us today rose from a storm of dust and noise. I went on reading Zola's novels for my own pleasure and instruction, but I must confess I faltered and gave up when I tackled the three tired and turgid volumes of the unfinished *Quatre Evangiles*, in which the old master had at last ground to a sad and boring halt. But everything he had written, the staggering number of tongues into which his work had been translated, fascinated me, and I discovered that many of his stories, including the three in this volume, were initially published in Russia, thanks to Ivan Turgenev. This came about in the following way.

In 1874 Zola was still a struggling writer. In that year the fourth volume in the ROUGON-

MACQUART series, *La conquête de Plassans,* was published, but apparently with little success. Flaubert, in a letter to Georges Sand, said that in six months it had sold only 1,700 copies and had not received a single review. Zola was debt-ridden and lived on a fixed salary paid to him by his publisher in lieu of royalties. This brought him the equivalent of a little less than fifteen dollars a week. Turgenev, who was living in Paris and knew how poor Zola was, arranged with Mikhail Stassyulevich, editor of the St. Petersburg journal *Vyestnik Evropy (The European Herald),* for Zola to contribute regularly to the paper. From 1874 to 1880, articles and stories by Zola appeared every month. '*Les coquillages de Monsieur Chabre*' was published as 'Sea-bathing in France' in September, 1876; '*Pour une nuit d'Amour*' as 'A Drama in a Country Town' the following month, and in November, 1877, '*Voyage circulaire*' came out as 'The Parisian on Holiday in the Country.'

This was the year during which Zola's luck turned and his fame and success began. On February 26, 1877, when he was thirty-seven, *L'Assommoir* was published and went through thirty-eight printings before the end of the year. As a result, his publisher drew up a new contract on a royalty basis. Zola's command of a larger audience also led to publication in French of some of those stories that had first appeared in Russia.

'*Pour une nuit d'amour*' ('For One Night of Love') was published in 1882 in a collection of stories entitled *Le Capitaine Durle*. It appeared again as a separate book in the Lotus Bleu collection in 1896, with a rivulet of type running between broad paper banks down a tiny page and with typically ninety-ish fuzzy illustrations by Georges Picard. The title page has a medallion drawing in pale blue of Thérèse de Marsanne riding on Colombel's back and plying her whip on that youth's masochistic shoulders. There is a pink frontispiece portrait of the imperious and heavy-browed heroine.

'*Voyage circulaire*' ('Round Trip') first appeared in French in 1929 in a posthumous collection of stories, *Madame Sourdis*; and '*Les coquillages de Monsieur Chabre*' was published with four other stories in *Naïs Micoulin* in 1884.

In England Zola's work was first made available through the devoted admiration and zealous energy of Henry Vizetelly, who, with the help of his son Ernest, translated nearly everything Zola wrote. In 1888 Vizetelly was sent to prison for three months for publishing, under the title *Soil*, his rendering into English of *La Terre*, which was condemned as 'obscene.' In the same year he brought out his own translation of a selection of stories, including the two longer ones in this volume, under the title *A*

17

Soldier's Honour, which appears never to have been reissued. Although he had great courage and enthusiasm, Vizetelly, as Angus Wilson has pointed out in his excellent *Emile Zola: an Introductory Study of His Novels* (revised edition, 1964, Secker and Warburg, London) was 'in his approach to his own work as translator, disarmingly modest, for he confessed that most of it was of poor quality, overhurriedly performed to meet debts or the demands of publishers who cared about novelty rather than quality....' But he carried on, even though some of his translations had to be bowdlerized to avoid further prosecution and appear under another imprint because he lacked the money to publish them himself.

This, then, was the background to the first publication and translations of these three stories, written before Zola became an international figure. What echoes and similarities are there in his other work?

'For One Night of Love' is a deliberately horrifying story of murder resulting from sexual license. Throughout all his work, Zola's puritanism led him to denounce the perils of sex, and his sensualism colored the risks he described. In May, 1867, *Thérèse Raquin* was published. This other Thérèse resembled Thérèse de Marsanne in more than name; but whereas Thérèse Raquin's lover Laurent is driven by lust for her to kill her husband Camille, Thérèse de Marsanne, gripped by the fury of her perverted nature, kills her lover with her own hands. Camille is drowned by his wife and her lover in a river; Colombel is tumbled into the Chanteclair as a corpse by his would-be successor in Thérèse's bed. But while Thérèse Raquin and Laurent are haunted and harried to suicide by the consequences of their lustful crime, Thérèse de Marsanne goes scot-free to enter into an arranged and loveless marriage to a 'suitable' husband before the eyes of those who admire her maidenly demeanor. By sparing her the retribution she deserved, Zola directed his barbs against her Catholic education, her noble status, and the stupidity of those of all classes who were deceived by her.

Nana appeared in 1880, and there is an interesting parallel—and some equally interesting differences—between the passage in which Nana climbs on the back of her distinguished and aristocratic lover Muffat and rides him across the room, and Thérèse's fetishist mounting of Colombel to spur him through the hidden paths of the garden of the château.

Nana had risen from slum poverty by the shrewd exploitation of her sexual charms to dominate men of political importance and distinction, and displayed in a crude and realistic way the extent of her domination. Thérèse de

Marsanne, on the other hand, belonged to a noble family in which there was a streak of madness and perversion. She exercised her sadism on a social and physical inferior until he, the perfect masochistic partner, had suffered sufficiently as her steed to bolt with her, throw her to the ground, and rape her. They now played new and adult roles and were welded into a struggling pair of demoniac lovers. Later, she calculatingly used her sexual allure to attract to her a humble post office employee, to whom she offered her body in return for his disposal of the corpse of her lover. There are therefore both moral and social differences between the prostitute Nana, straddling and straddled by French society, and Thérèse, who uses her humble admirers for the furtherance and concealment of her perverted desires.

'Round Trip,' compared with the immense bulk of Zola's detailed and highly-colored oil paintings of French society, is an affectionate and gay etching. One can almost see it as a short film in the manner of Renoir or Tati. In fact, Zola's novels and stories are all highly cinematic in conception and execution.

In this story there are the initial thrusts against the cash-conscious mother, for whom centimes and francs have long since taken the place of kisses and love-making, the embodiment of the grasping shopkeeper, and against the *comme il faut* train passengers who frown on the young couple's public tokens of affection. There is the father-in-law, also a shopkeeper, but one who is capable, one feels, of a vigorous flirtation on the side despite his enervating talk of the architectural delights of the tour. And there are all the sad-comic (as distinct from sick-comic) touches of the single beds, the too-thin walls in the hotels, ending in the train's momentary halt at a kind of French Adlestrop, which Edward Thomas remembered because

'. . . one afternoon
of heat the express-train drew up there
unwontedly . . .'

But this was France, and *'un trou adorable de verdure perdu dans les arbres,'* 'an enchanting green arbor hidden by trees,' and some forty years before Edward Thomas wrote his poem. The young couple might not have found such a pleasant inn at Adlestrop in which to spend the remainder of their honeymoon in idyllic solitude. In this story the forceful proselytizing genius of Zola drew up, like the train, unwontedly, at a whistle stop of amused and touching tenderness.

There is also tenderness in *'Monsieur Chabre,'* but of a different kind. This is no etching. This is Zola in action with a full palette, painting the vivid and dramatic Atlantic coastline with giant strokes on the granite cliffs. This background of caves and cliffs, tides and shell-fish, with the characters of the plodding, worrying cuckolded husband who so richly deserves his horns, and the handsome, youthful giant who sports with the beautiful and unfulfilled young woman in the sea, pursues her across the damp sands that terrify the timid husband, and eventually mates with her to the sound of the sea while her husband on the cliffs above fortifies his virility with winkles—all this unrolls with the inevitability of a myth or a folk tale. But if there is a legendary quality in the evocation of towering pillars of rock, crystal pools, and waving seaweed, there is at times also something of the comic seaside postcard. Then the aging thalassophobe, with the wife who is part Atalanta and part naiad, becomes 'timid, middle-aged party' sweating in the sun while his nubile wife disports herself in the sea with 'handsome young local man.' It is impossible to resist the idea that a suitable legend for such a postcard would be 'cuckolds and muscles.'

Edmund Gosse, in his preface to Zola's *Attack on the Mill,* which was published in 1892, referred to both *'Pour une nuit d'Amour'* and *'Les coquillages de Monsieur Chabre,'* and it is amusing to see what he had to say: 'As to *"Pour une nuit d'Amour,"* it is not needful to do more than say that it is one of the most repulsive productions ever published by its author, and a vivid exception to the general innocuous character of his short stories . . . . In *"Les coquillages de Monsieur Chabre,"* which I confess I read when it first appeared, and have now reread with amusement, we see the heavy M. Zola endeavoring to sport as gracefully as M. de Maupassant, and in the same style. The impression of buoyant Atlantic seas and hollow caverns is well rendered in this most unedifying story.'

Zola never wrote another story in quite the same vein as 'Monsieur Chabre.' Here the bourgeois husband gets his desserts, adultery goes unpunished. Estelle is depicted as a wholesome and healthy young woman and not as a scheming sensualist. Hector is no sinister seducer, but a fine upstanding young man bearing impeccable manners and gifts of seafood. He and Estelle enjoy each other without *arrière pensée* or fear of retribution, and Monsieur Chabre gets his long-awaited heir. All ends happily, without either condemnation or catastrophe. Estelle is more *fille mal gardée* than bartered bride, and what Monsieur Chabre's eye does not see, his heart will not grieve for.

These three stories show three expressions on the faces of love. All three portraits are signed with the force and clarity of Emile Zola's artistic genius.

R.G.

FOR ONE NIGHT OF LOVE

I

THE little town of P— stands on a hill. Below its ancient walls a deep stream flows between steep banks. It is called the Chanteclair and undoubtedly got its name from the rippling sound of its water. If you come from the south by the Versailles road you cross the Chanteclair by a single-arch bridge whose low, broad sides are used as seats by the old men of the town. The road from the bridge leads directly into the Rue Beau-Soleil, which goes up to the Place des Quatre-Femmes, where coarse grass grows between the large paving stones and masks them with a meadow greenness. The houses are wrapped in silence. Every half hour or so, the lagging step of a passer-by starts a dog barking behind a stable door, and the only excitement —twice daily—is the steady tread of the officers who go for their meals to a pension in the Rue Beau-Soleil.

Julien Michon lived in a house on the left-hand side of the street, belonging to a gardener. He rented a big room on the first floor, and as the gardener lived in the other side of the house, overlooking the Rue Catherine, Julien was left to himself, with his own stairway and door. At twenty-five, Julien was as set in his ways as any retired middle-class citizen.

In the old days the Michons were harness-makers at Alluets near Mantes. After their death —and Julien's parents died when he was very young—an uncle sent Julien to a boarding school. When he too died, Julien had to earn a living and for the past five years had been a clerk in the post office at P—. He earned a very small wage and had no prospect of a raise. Yet he managed to save a little and considered himself lucky.

Julien was tall, big-boned, and very self-conscious of his large hands. He felt that he was ugly, his head too square and like a sculpture left unpolished and roughly finished by an inexperienced sculptor. Therefore he was shy and particularly so toward girls. He remembered with embarrassment that a laundress had once laughingly told him that he was not too bad. He walked with dangling arms, hunched back, and bent head, striding along as though he wanted to catch up with his own shadow. His awkwardness gave him a perpetually alarmed air and an unhealthy wish to bury himself in ordinariness and self-effacement. He seemed resigned to growing older in his own way, without friends and without a girl, like a cloistered monk.

But the existence he led did not seem to weigh on his broad shoulders. Julien was very happy in his own way. His outlook on life was calm and uncomplicated. He went about his daily work, with its set routine, in a straightforward way. He left each morning and applied himself to his job just as he had done the previous day. He lunched on a sandwich, went back to work, later returned home, had his supper, retired to bed, and slept. The following day he did the same things, and so on throughout the week, and for months on end. This routine eventually lulled him into the same way of life as that of oxen dragging carts during the daytime and resting at night in clean straw. He endured with pleasure the monotony of the life he led. After dinner he often liked to walk down the Rue Beau-Soleil and sit on the bridge until nine o'clock. With his legs dangling over the water, he enjoyed watching the River Chanteclair below and listening to the whisper of its silver ripples. The water reflected the willows overhanging from the banks, and twilight filled the sky with an ashy softness. Julien loved the surrounding calm and felt that the Chanteclair shared his contentment as it flowed ceaselessly and silently along its appointed course. When the stars came out he went home to bed, replete with the freshness of the evening.

Julien had other distractions. On public holidays he went walking for long distances and returned worn out. He made friends with a dumb man, a printer's engraver, with whom he would walk for a whole afternoon without their exchanging even a sign. And sometimes he went to the Café des Voyageurs and played draughts with his dumb friend, games that were both slow and thoughtful. At one time he kept a dog, but it was run over by a carriage, and his affection for it was so deep and lasting that he could never again bring himself to have a pet at home.

His colleagues at the post office used to tease him about a ragged and barefoot little girl of about ten who sold boxes of matches. He gave her money but always left the matches, and took good care to be out of sight when he did so because the others' teasing annoyed him. He had never been seen in the company of a girl on the walks above the town walls. Even the working girls of P—, who were by no means slow in coming forward, decided in the end to leave him in peace, once they had seen him frozen with embarrassment because he took their laughing encouragement for mockery. Some of the townspeople called him stupid, while others maintained that a sharp eye should be kept on such boys, with their gentle airs and solitary habits.

Julien's sole refuge and the only place where he could breathe freely was his room. There he felt safely shut away from people. He could hold up his head, laugh out loud, and catching sight of himself in his looking glass, be surprised at how young he looked. His room was very big and he had moved into it a large sofa, a round table, two upright chairs, and an armchair. But there was still plenty of space to walk around; his bed stood unseen in a deep alcove, and a walnut dressing chest between two windows looked like a toy. Whether walking around or lying down, he never tired of his own company. Once he left his office, he never set pen to paper and decided that reading tired him. The old woman who ran the place he went to for his meals persisted in trying to educate him and lent him novels that he took back to her without being able to remember a thing about plots he found too complicated and, to his way of thinking, lacking in common sense. He used to draw a little, always the same profile of a woman with a stern expression, her braids twisted around her head and pearls wound into her hair. His only passion was music, and for whole evenings at a time he played the flute. This, more than anything, was his great relaxation.

Julien's playing was self-taught. For a long time one of his dearest ambitions had been to buy a flute of yellow wood from a junk dealer in the market place. He had the money but dared not go into the shop for fear of looking ridiculous. At last he plucked up enough courage one evening to buy it, and hurried off with the flute held tight beneath his overcoat. For two years, with doors and windows carefully closed so that he should not be overheard, he went over and over again an old teaching manual that he had picked up in a little bookshop. It was only during the past six months that he had dared play with the window open. He could only play tunes, slow and simple romantic airs, a century old, which were unbearably tender as he played them with the clumsiness of a novice bursting with feeling. During the warm evenings when the neighborhood was asleep, the sound of the flute floated from the big candlelit room like a soft vibrating voice that spoke of love to the lonely night—not daring to do so in the daytime.

If Julien played a tune he knew by heart he would often blow out the light and play in the dark, so saving on the candles. Passers-by used to look up, wondering whence came this frail, pleasing sound, not unlike the song of a distant nightingale. As the old yellow wood of the flute was slightly cracked, it had a rather muted tone, like the still, innocent voice of an old gentlewoman singing the minuets of her youth. One by one the notes took the air with a fragile, winged sound, as if the melody belonged to night itself, blending with the nocturnal sighs and shadows.

Julien was always afraid that the neighbors might complain. But the inhabitants of small country towns sleep soundly, and the only people whose houses gave on to the Place des Quatre-Femmes were a lawyer named Savour-nin and Captain Pidoux, a retired police officer. Both neighbors were in bed and asleep by nine o'clock. But Julien was more afraid of the people living in the big private house belonging to the Marsanne family, a house whose gray and dismal façade was directly in front of his windows, austere as a cloister. A flight of stone steps, green with grass, led up to a door with a rounded arch, studded with huge nails. It had only two stories and its ten windows were opened and closed at the same time each day without revealing a glimpse of the rooms that lay hidden behind tight-drawn thick curtains. On the left, the tall chestnut trees in the garden threw up a billow of green leaves that foamed to the eaves of the house. When Julien looked at this impressive mansion, with its private grounds, imposing walls, and air of majestic boredom, it seemed to him that the Marsannes only had to say the word to stop his playing the flute.

As Julien leaned on his window sill and looked out at the sprawling grandeur of it all, he had an almost religious feeling about the building and its grounds. The Marsannes' house was famous in the district, and it was said that visitors from far-off places came to see it. There were also stories about the Marsanne fortune. For a long time Julien stared at the old house in an attempt to fathom the mysteries of that all-powerful wealth. But in the hours he spent dreaming at this window, all he could see were the gray walls and the dark spread of the chestnut trees.

Nobody ever walked down the uneven stone steps, and the great mossy door was never opened; it had been closed when the Marsannes took to using a side gate on the Rue Saint-Anne. There was another entrance at the far end of an alley near the town walls. This led into the garden, but Julien could not see it from his bedroom. It seemed to him that the house was as dead as one of those fairy-tale palaces inhabited by invisible people. He could just see, each morning and evening, the arms of a servant who opened and closed the shutters, and then the house lapsed once again into its usual melancholy look of a neglected tomb in a churchyard. The branches of the chestnuts spread so low and thick that they hid the paths in the garden. The impression of being near a hermetically sealed existence, haughty and silent, sharpened the young man's excitement. So that was wealth? A sad kind of peace, which gave you the same sort of religious shivers as a church vault!

He often stayed at his window for an hour at a time after blowing out his candle, in the hope of probing the secrets of the Marsannes. At night the house stood out against the sky as a dark silhouette and the chestnuts cast their inky shadow against it. The curtains must have been very carefully drawn, because no chink of light showed through the shutters. The house even seemed to be without that kind of breathing inhabited houses have, in which the breath of sleeping people can be sensed. It melted completely into the darkness of night; and it was then that Julien took heart to play boldly. He was able to trill away without hindrance and the empty house opposite echoed the pearl-like notes. Slow passages trickled away into the shadows of the garden, where you could have heard a pin drop. The old yellow wood seemed to play its ancient airs before Sleeping Beauty's castle.

One Sunday, when Julien was in the square where the church stood, a colleague from the post office pointed out to him a tall old man and an old woman: the Marquis and Marquise de Marsanne. Julien had never seen them before, since they went out so rarely. He was strangely moved by the thin and solemn couple who walked with measured tread and acknowledged obsequious greetings with a slight nod. Julien's companion told him that they had a daughter,

Mademoiselle Thérèse de Marsanne, who was still at convent school. He added that young Colombel, Monsieur Savournin's clerk, was the son of Thérèse's wet nurse. As the old couple turned into the Rue Saint-Anne, Colombel went up to them and the Marquis shook hands with him, an honor he had not granted to anyone else in the street that morning. It cut Julien to the quick because Colombel, a youth of twenty with clever eyes and a peevish mouth, was an old enemy. He used to tease Julien about his shyness and set the laundresses of the Rue Beau-Soleil on him, to such an extent that the two boys fought one day and the lawyer's clerk collected a pair of black eyes.

That Sunday evening, recalling what he had learned in the morning about the Marsannes, Julien played his flute more softly than ever. Yet his preoccupation with the Marsanne house did not upset his daily habits, which were as regular as clockwork. He went to his office, lunched and supped, and took a walk along the bank of the Chanteclair, and eventually the silent house became a part of his quiet life. After two years he had grown so used to the grass in the cracks of the stone steps and the gray wall of the house with the black shutters, that they fell into place with everything and merged with the neighborhood.

Julien had been living in the Place des Quatre-

Femmes for five years when something happened one July evening that changed his whole life. It was warm, and the sky was bright with stars. He was playing in the dark without paying much attention to what he was doing, lingering on certain notes and changing tempi, when suddenly a window in the Marsanne house opened and stayed open, lighting up the gray wall. A young girl leaned on the sill, in profile, as if she were listening. Julien trembled and stopped playing. He could not see the girl's face clearly, but only her shoulder-length hair. A soft voice floated over to him out of the silence.

'Did you hear that, Françoise? It sounded like music.'

'Perhaps it was just a nightingale, mademoiselle,' replied a rough voice from inside the room. 'Close the window, and mind the insects don't get in.'

When the house was once more shrouded in darkness, Julien sat in his chair, his eyes still seeing the square of light that had appeared in a wall which, until then, had seemed dead. He shivered, wondering whether or not he should be pleased by what he had seen. An hour went by and then he began to play again, very softly, and smiling at the idea that the girl probably thought it was a nightingale singing in the chestnut trees.

II

Next day everyone at the post office was talking about Mademoiselle Thérèse de Marsanne having come home from convent school. Julien did not mention that he had seen her, with her hair hanging loose about her shoulders. He was very perturbed and had a peculiar, undefinable resentment against this girl who would upset his habits. That window opposite, which might open at any moment, was certainly going to be a nuisance. He would no longer feel at home; a man at the window would have been preferable because a woman was always more ready to make fun of you. How could he go on with the flute now? He played too badly for the ears of a young lady who had surely studied music. By evening, after thinking about it all day, he was convinced that he detested Thérèse.

Julien crept home furtively that day and did not light a candle when he went into his room, so that she would not see him. He was so bad tempered that he thought of going to bed at once. But the wish to know what was going on in the house opposite was too strong. The window stayed shut. At about ten o'clock, only a pale gleam showed between the slats of the shutters, and when it went out he was left staring at a dark rectangle.

Each evening, from then on, he took up his reluctant watch. He spied on the house and noticed, as he had done when he first lived there, every puff of breeze that brushed against the silent old stones. Nothing seemed to have changed and the house appeared to be sunk in the same profound sleep as before. Only by straining his eyes and ears could he sense the new life that had entered it. Sometimes it was a light moving behind the windowpanes, the edge of a curtain not tightly drawn, a glimpse of an enormous room. At other times he caught the sound of a light step in the garden, of a distant piano accompanying a voice, or of even fainter noises betraying the presence of youth within the ancient walls. Julien explained his curiosity to himself by pretending that the noises disturbed him. How he missed the old days, when the empty house echoed the music of his flute!

Although he would not admit it to himself, one of his deepest wishes was to see Thérèse again. He saw in his mind's eye a pink face, a mischievous expression, and sparkling eyes. But since he never dared look out of his window in the daytime, he merely had a glimpse of her at night, in deep shadow.

One morning, as he was opening his shutters to let in the sun, he saw Thérèse standing in the middle of her room. He stood stock still, not daring to move. She was tall and pale, with regular and beautiful features, and seemed lost in thought. She was so different from the picture he had formed of her that he was almost frightened. Her mouth was wide, with very red lips, and her deep-set eyes, dark and expressionless, gave her a cruel and regal look. She crossed slowly to the window, appearing not to see him, as if he were too far, too remote from her. As she moved away, there was so much grace and strength in the rhythmical swaying of her neck that Julien, despite his broad shoulders, felt as weak as a child by comparison. When he got to know her she alarmed him even more.

Henceforth the young man led a miserable existence. This beautiful girl with her serious and patrician expression, who was living so near him, drove him to despair. She never looked at him, she ignored his presence. But the thought that she might notice him and find him ridiculous made him shudder. His pathological shyness led him to believe that her every movement was calculated to make fun of him. He took to slinking home with his shoulders hunched and, once in his room, he took good care not to move around. Why didn't she look at him? She walked to her window, glanced at the dark stones below, and then turned away without suspecting that he was anxiously watching from the other side of the square. And just as he had once trembled at the idea that she might see him, so now he shivered with the desire to feel her gaze upon him. His every thought was of her.

When Thérèse rose in the morning, Julien, who had always been punctual, forgot about his office. Her pale face and red lips still frightened him, but now he enjoyed the feeling of fear. Hidden behind a curtain, he let himself be filled with the terror she inspired in him until he felt faint and his legs trembled as though he had walked a long way. In his daydreams he imagined that she suddenly noticed him and that his fear vanished because she smiled at him.

He then had the notion of winning her over with music. On warm evenings he began playing again. He left the window wide open and, in the dark, played the oldest tunes he knew— pastorales as simple as the part songs that girls sing. Lingering tremolo notes followed one another like lovesick ladies of another age dancing with their skirts outspread. He played on moonless nights and when the square was in darkness, so that nobody could tell whence came the soft music that brushed the sleeping houses with the gentleness of a night bird's wing. One evening, he had the thrill of seeing Thérèse, dressed in white, lean on her window sill at bedtime, listening to the same music she had heard on the day she returned home.

'Listen to that, Françoise,' she said in her deep voice. 'It can't be a bird, can it?'

'Oh,' replied an elderly woman whose shadow Julien could just see, 'it's probably a street musician playing down in the town somewhere.'

'Yes, it's very far off,' said the young girl after a moment's silence, cooling her arms on the sill in the evening breeze.

After this Julien played louder in the evenings. The fever in his blood rounded the notes and pulsed through the old yellow wood of the flute. Thérèse listened each night and wondered about the elusive music that danced to her ears from rooftop to rooftop once darkness had fallen. One evening the music was so close that it washed over her, and she guessed that it came from one of the old, sleeping houses in the square. Julien played with all the passionate feeling of which he was capable, and the flute vibrated with notes of tinkling crystal. The dark lent him such courage that he hoped to attract her by the sound of his music. And Thérèse did, in fact, lean out of her window as if she were drawn and won over by it.

'Come inside,' said the old woman. 'It's stormy and you'll have nightmares.'

Julien could not sleep that night. He imagined

that Thérèse had guessed his feelings and might even have seen him. As he tossed and turned feverishly in his bed, he wondered if he should show himself as the window the next day. It seemed ridiculous to go on hiding now. But he decided against it and was standing at his window at six the following morning, putting his flute back in its case, when Thérèse's window opened.

Usually Thérèse never rose until eight, but there she was, in a dressing gown and with her hair braided at the nape of her neck, leaning on her window sill. Julien stared stupidly at her, unable to turn away and with his hands fumbling with the flute he was trying to take apart. Thérèse stared back with a steady and imperious look. For a moment she seemed to be taking him in—his great, bony, rough-hewn body that gave him the ugliness of a shy giant. She was no longer the excited young girl of whom he had caught a glimpse the previous evening. Now she had a haughty air; she was very pale and her lips were very red. When she had finished studying him with the detached air with which she would have summed up a dog on the footpath, had her opinion been asked, the slight pursing of her lips expressed her disapproval and, turning her back on him, she closed the window.

With legs trembling, Julien collapsed into a

chair, babbling to himself.

'Oh, my God! She doesn't like me! And I love her so much, I'll die!'

He put his head in his hands and sobbed. That was what came of letting himself be seen. When one is awkward and shambling, it is better to keep out of sight and not frighten young girls. He cursed himself, furious at his ugliness. He should have gone on playing the flute in the dark, like a night bird that charms with its song, and never have shown himself in the light of day if he wanted to please her. Then he would have remained for her a soft music, just an old melody of a mysterious love. Then, too, she would have adored him without knowing him, like a kind of Prince Charming come from afar to die of love beneath her window. But he, rough and stupid Julien, had broken the spell. Now that she knew him to be as coarse as an ox, she would nevermore like the music he played.

And indeed, although he went on playing his most tender airs and chose the warm nights filled with the scent of flowers and leaves, Thérèse no longer listened, no longer heard him. She walked back and forth in her room and leaned on her window sill as if he were not there in the house opposite, telling of his love in humble notes. There was even a time when she exclaimed, 'Oh, that out-of-tune flute gets on my nerves!'

Julien, in despair, threw the flute into a drawer and gave up playing.

Young Colombel too, jeered at Julien. As he was going to his office one day, he had looked up and seen Julien practicing at his window. Ever since then, Colombel had laughed sarcastically whenever he crossed the square. Julien knew that Colombel was invited to the Marsannes' house; and that was a heart-rending thought—not because Julien was jealous of the little creature, but because he would have given his life's blood to be in his place for just one hour.

Colombel's mother, old Françoise, had been in the household for years. She had suckled Thérèse as a baby and now she was her personal maid. The child of noble family and the little peasant boy had grown up together, and it was quite natural that something of their childhood friendship should have remained. But this did nothing to lessen Julien's suffering when he met Colombel in the street and saw his thin-lipped smile. His antipathy increased from the day he realized that the skinny youth was rather good-looking. He had a face like a cat, delicate, pretty, and devilish, with green eyes and a slight beard curling on his soft chin. If only Julien could have pushed him into a corner of the ramparts, he would have made him pay dearly for his luck in visiting Thérèse at home!

A year went by. Julien was very unhappy. He lived only for Thérèse. His heart was locked in that cold house across the way and he was dying of love and his own clumsiness. Whenever he had a moment to spare, he went to his room and stared across at the gray wall whose every patch of moss he knew by heart. During those long months he had strained both eyes and ears, yet still had no idea of the kind of life that went on in the grim house that had become the prison of his soul. He was thrown into confusion by the slightest sounds and the smallest glimmers of light. What was going on? A celebration or a funeral? He could never tell, because only the front of the house, on the other side, gave any sign of life. According to whether he was sad or happy he daydreamed whatever he wished: the boisterous games played by Thérèse and Colombel, the young girl strolling beneath the branches of the chestnuts, the dancing that placed her in the arms of her partners, her sudden melancholic moods that sent her to her shuttered room to sit and weep. Or perhaps all he heard were the mincing steps of the Marquis and Marquise crossing the old floors like mice. He really knew nothing; all he had before his eyes was Thérèse's window set in that mysterious wall. Every day she came to the window, as silent as the stone itself, and never once did her appearance there give him cause for hope. He was filled with dismay when he thought how unknown and distant she was to him.

Julien's happiest moments were the days when the window remained open. Then he could see every corner of the room while Thérèse was out of it. It took him six months to discover that her bed was in an alcove to the left and that it had pink silk curtains. Then, after a further six months, he saw that opposite the bed was a Louis Quinze chest with a looking glass in a china frame on top of it. There was also a white marble fireplace. The room became Julien's dream paradise.

His love for her was torn in all directions. For weeks on end he hid himself, ashamed of his ugliness. Then, in all his feverish longing, he was rent by anger and the wish to show her his strong limbs and irregular features. Again, for weeks at a time, he went to his window, wearing her down with his steady stare. On two occasions he blew kisses to her, with that roughness of which shy people are capable when they are carried away by a sudden gust of audacity.

Thérèse was not even annoyed. While he watched her from his hiding place, she went to and fro with the same regal expression and, when he came into view, she looked no different, only haughtier and colder. He never caught her in an unguarded moment. If their eyes met, she was in no hurry to turn away. When he heard in the

47

post office that Mademoiselle de Marsanne was very devout and kind, he protested silently. No, she was not religious at all, she was ruled only by the pulsing of her blood and that was why she had bright red lips; the pallor of her face was the result of the contempt with which she treated everyone. Then he would weep because he had insulted her and he begged her forgiveness, as though she were a saint wrapped in the purity of her own wings.

During that first year, the days went by without bringing any change in the situation. When summer came around again, Julien was disturbed by a strange feeling. The same things happened each day, shutters opening in the morning and closing at evening, and her regular appearances. Yet there was the hint of something new from her room. Thérèse was both paler and taller. One day, in a feverish moment, he dared once more to blow a kiss from the tips of his burning fingers. She stared fixedly at him in her disturbing way without leaving her window and it was Julien who turned away with a crimson face.

Toward the end of summer something happened that shook Julien deeply, although it was quite ordinary. Almost every day at twilight Thérèse's window, which had been left ajar, was closed so roughly that both wood and fastener creaked. Each time Julien started violently, racked by doubts and deeply troubled in heart without knowing why. After this sudden clatter, the house relapsed into such a deathly silence that he was afraid. For a long time he was unable to see whose hands closed the window, but one evening he saw Thérèse's pale hands snatch at the fastening with angry impatience. Then, an hour later, when she opened it again, she did so slowly and listlessly, pausing a moment to rest her elbows on the sill. Then she paced slowly throughout her room, with all its virginal purity, preoccupied with the sweet nothings that young girls think about. Julien remained without a thought in his head, but with the creaking of the window latches constantly in his ears.

One autumn evening, when the weather was mild and the sky overcast, he heard the shutter creak more violently than usual. Julien shuddered and tears coursed down his cheeks without his knowing why, as he sat facing the dismal walls fading into the shadows of twilight. That morning it had rained and the half-bare chestnut trees had a smell of death about them.

Yet Julien waited for the window to open again. And suddenly it did, as abruptly as it had closed. Thérèse stood there. She was very pale, wide-eyed and with her hair falling about her face. She stayed in front of the open window and blew a kiss to Julien, touching her scarlet mouth with the tips of all ten fingers.

In his dismay, he clasped both hands to his chest, as though asking if that kiss were meant for him.

Thérèse thought he was retreating and she leaned farther out, placed her fingers to her lips again, and blew him a second kiss. Then a third —as though she were sending back to Julien the three kisses he had sent to her. He stood open-mouthed, staring at her framed there by her window in the pale twilight.

When she thought she had convinced him, she glanced down into the little square and said in a stifled voice,

'Come.'

He went down and walked toward the Marsanne house. As he looked up, a door was opened —that same door that had been bolted for perhaps half a century and the hinges of which were thick with lichen. He walked in a stupor, no longer surprised at anything. The moment he entered the house, the door closed and a small icy hand took his and led him up a flight of stairs, along a corridor, through a room, and into another that he recognized at once. He stood in that dreamed-of paradise, the room with the pink silk bed curtains. The sun was setting slowly. He wanted to fall to his knees but Thérèse stood straight before him, her hands clasped firmly and so resolute that she suppressed the shiver that almost ran through her.

'Do you love me?' she demanded in a low voice.

'Yes, yes,' he stammered.

She made a sign with one hand, forbidding him to waste words. She continued in a haughty voice that lent her words a chaste sincerity becoming to the lips of a young girl.

'If I gave myself to you, you would do anything I ask, would you not?'

He was unable to reply, but merely clasped his hands. He would have sold his soul for a single kiss.

'Well, then, I want you to do something for me.'

Since he still stood in a daze, she spoke with sudden violence, feeling that she was near the end of her strength and that she might not risk going further.

'Look here, you must swear to me first. I'll keep my side of the bargain. Swear, swear to me now!'

'I promise. Yes, anything you wish,' he said with complete abandon.

The scene of her room intoxicated him. The bed curtains were drawn and the mere thought of that chaste bed in the soft shadow of the pink hangings filled him with an almost religious ecstasy. Then, with suddenly brutal hands, she tore open the curtains and revealed the alcove lit by the sinister fading light of evening. The bed was in disorder, the sheets trailing, and a pillow on the floor looked as though a hole had been bitten in it. Across the rumpled lace-edged bedclothes, there sprawled the barefoot body of a man.

'There,' she said in a strangled voice, 'that man was my lover. I pushed him, he fell, and I don't know what happened. Anyway, he's dead and you've got to get him out of here. Do you understand? That's all there is to it, so there you are.'

III

When she was a small girl, Thérèse de Marsanne bullied Colombel. He was barely six months older than she, and Françoise, her wet nurse, had raised her son—with some difficulty —on a nursing bottle. As he grew up in the house, he later found himself in a vague relationship, somewhere between servant and playmate, to the little girl.

Thérèse was a difficult child. She was, however, neither noisy nor a tomboy. Far from it— she was strangely serious in manner and led those visitors to whom she dropped low curtsies into believing she was a model child. But she did odd things. She would suddenly shout incoherently and stamp furiously when she was alone, or lie flat on her back in the middle of a garden path, obstinately refusing to get up despite the slaps she was given.

Nobody knew what went on in her mind. She already veiled any expression in her eyes, and instead of those calm pools in which one sees the souls of little girls, there was an inky darkness in which it was impossible to read anything.

From the age of six, she began torturing Colombel. He was sickly and small for his years. She used to lead him to the foot of the garden to a place under the chestnut trees and, hidden by branches, leap on his back and make him carry her. She would ride him around in a circle for an hour at a time, squeezing his neck, digging her heels into his ribs, without stopping to let him get his breath back. He was the horse and she was the lady rider. When he stumbled and seemed fit to drop, she bit his ear until it bled, gripping him so furiously that her little nails dug into his flesh. And the gallop would begin again, with the cruel little six-year-old queen, her hair streaming behind her as they sped between the trees, riding on the back of the small boy, whom she treated like a beast of burden.

Later, in the presence of her parents, she pinched him and forbade him to cry out, threatening to have him sent out of the house if he dared mention the games they played. A kind of secret life sprang up between them, a way of being together that changed when they were with other people. If they were alone, she treated him like a toy that she wanted to break to see what was inside. For wasn't she a marquise, used to seeing people at her feet? And as she had been given a little man to play with, she could do whatever she wanted with him. As she got bored with bullying Colombel when they were out of sight, she invented the added pleasure of kicking him or sticking a pin in his arm when they were among others, mesmerizing him to such an extent with her big solemn eyes that he did not even wince.

Colombel endured his martyrdom with a silent rebellion that often made him tremble with the wish to strangle his young mistress, before he could master his feelings and hide them in his downcast eyes. But Colombel, too, had a sly temperament. He did not actually dislike being beaten and even got a bitter kind of pleasure out of it. Sometimes he deliberately allowed himself to be pricked and, trembling violently, waited for the thrust of the pin. And, when its point pierced his flesh, felt a sense of real fulfillment as he gave himself up to the delights of resentment. He began to take his revenge by falling on stones, dragging Thérèse down with him, heedless of the risk of breaking a leg and delighted when she got bruised. If he refused to cry out when she pricked him in front of others, it was so that nobody should come between them. What went on between them was strictly their affair, a struggle from which he felt he would eventually emerge victorious.

The Marquis was concerned about this violent streak in his daughter's character. He said that she took after one of her uncles, who led a wild and adventurous life until he was murdered in a sordid district. A thread of tragedy ran through the history of the Marsannes, a strange twist through their arrogant and distinguished line, handed on down the ages. It was like a touch of madness or a form of perversion, a faulty streak that looked for a time as though it might be the end of the family. The Marquis therefore assumed that he was doing the right thing when he sent Thérèse to a convent school where she would be subjected to a strict discipline that he hoped would make her more tractable. She stayed at the convent until she was eighteen.

When Thérèse returned home, she was well-behaved and very tall. Her parents were pleased by her apparent piety. In church, she sat with her forehead bent over clasped hands. At home, she radiated innocence and peace. Her only fault was greediness. From morn to night she ate sweets, sucking them avidly and half-closing her eyes at the same time. Nobody would have recognized the sullen and stubborn child who had once come in from the garden with her clothes in tatters, refusing to say how she got into such a mess. The Marquis and Marquise had kept closed house for fifteen years and they now thought about inviting people again. They gave dinners for their aristocratic neighbors and even held a ball now and then. They hoped to find a husband for their daughter, but although she was well-mannered, well-dressed, and danced well, there was something in the expression on her pale face that alarmed the young men who fell in love with her.

Since her return, Thérèse had never once mentioned Colombel. The Marquis had kept an eye on him and placed him in Monsieur Savournin's office after having attended to his education. One day Françoise brought her son to the house and pushed him forward, presenting him to Thérèse and reminding her that they used to be playmates. Colombel smiled, was very neat and clean, and showed no trace of embarrassment. Thérèse stared calmly at him, said that of course she remembered him, and then turned away. But a week later Colombel was back and he soon slipped into his old position in the house. Each evening, after leaving his office, he went there with music and books. Nobody paid very much attention to him and he was given the run of the house as if he were a servant or a poor relation. He was one of the family's responsibilities. And so he was left alone with the young girl without anyone giving it a second thought. Just as they had done when they were children, so now they shut themselves in the large rooms or stayed for hours in shady hidden corners of the garden. But they no longer played the same games. Thérèse sauntered around, her skirts swishing against the grass, and Colombel, dressed like a rich young man about town, walked beside her, prodding the ground now and then with the Malacca cane he always carried.

Yet once more she became queen and he, her slave. True, she no longer bit him, but she had a way of walking at his side that made him seem smaller and smaller, changing him into a court lackey holding his sovereign's train. She tormented him with her capricious moods, talking affectionately and then, as the whim struck her, switching to a stony hardness. For his part, Colombel—once she turned her head—shot glances at her as bright and sharp as the edge of a sword, and his whole twisted personality was coiled as he watched and planned treachery.

One summer evening, after they had been walking for a long time in the shade of the chestnut trees, Thérèse thought for a moment and then said, very seriously, 'You know, Colombel, I'm tired. Suppose you carry me like you used to. Remember?'

He laughed lightly and then replied, in the same serious tone, 'If you like, Thérèse.'

But she began walking again and merely replied, 'All right. I just wanted to know.'

They continued their stroll. Night fell and the shadows lay dark beneath the branches. They were talking about a woman in the town who had married an officer. As they turned into a narrower path, Colombel was about to step back so that she could pass in front of him when she pushed him violently and made him go first. They both fell silent.

Suddenly Thérèse leaped onto his back with the same agility as when she was a small, wild girl.

'Come on! Get going!' she said in a different voice, choked with the same violence she had shown as a child.

She snatched his cane and beat his thighs with it. Clutching his shoulders and almost suffocating him with the nerve-tightened grip of a rider's legs, she drove him crazily into the black shadows of the bushes. She went on beating him, guiding his course so that he should go as fast as possible. The sound of his headlong gallop was muted by the grass. He had not said a single word; he panted deeply, bracing himself on his short, slender legs beneath the tall young girl's warm weight around his neck.

But when she cried out 'That's enough,' he did not stop. He galloped even faster, as though carried on by his own momentum. With his hands clasped behind him, he held her so tightly by the thighs that she could not jump off. Now the horse was running away from its mistress. Suddenly, despite the scourging cane and her searing nails, he careered toward a gardener's tool shed. There he threw her to the ground and raped her on the straw-littered floor. His turn to be master had come at last.

Thérèse grew paler, her lips redder, and the circles around her eyes darker. She continued her pious mode of life. A few days later the same thing happened again: she leaped onto Colombel's back, tried to master him, and finished by being thrown on the straw in the shed. In front of others, her attitude to him was unchanged—she still showed the kindness and condescension of an older sister. He, too, was still calm and smiling. They were once more just as they had been when they were six years old, like vicious animals that, the moment they were turned loose, fell to biting each other. But now, in the stormy moments of lust, it was the male who was the victor.

Their sexual relationship was terrifying. Thérèse let Colombel go to her bedroom. She had given him a key to the little garden door that led into the alley of the town ramparts. To reach her he had to pass through another room at night, the very room, in fact, where his mother slept. But the lovers displayed such calm audacity that they were never surprised. They even took to meeting in broad daylight. Colombel went to her before dinner and Thérèse closed the shutters against the neighbors' eyes. They were driven into each other's company at all hours, not in order to whisper those tender nothings that lovers of twenty exchange, but to continue the struggle between their respective prides.

They often fell to quarreling, insulting each other in low voices, trembling with temper the more because they could not give way to their urge to shout and fight aloud.

One evening, as he walked about in Thérèse's room, barefoot and in his shirt sleeves, it occurred to Colombel to pick her up in the way strong men in a fairground grasp their opponents at the start of a wrestling bout. Thérèse tried to free herself and said, 'Let me go. You know I'm stronger than you. I'll hurt you.'

'Go on then, hurt me,' he sniggered.

He always used to shake her to get the better of her. She, fighting back, would cross her arms and thrust back at him. They often did this through an impulse to struggle together. More often than not, it was Colombel who fell backward onto the carpet, choking, limp, and helpless. He was too short and she could pick him up and crush him to her as if she were a giantess.

But on this particular evening, Thérèse slipped to her knees and Colombel, with a rapid movement, knocked her flat and stood triumphantly over her.

'There you are, you see. You're not stronger than I,' he sneered.

She turned white with fury. Rising slowly to her feet, she grabbed him without a word but with such trembling anger that he shuddered. She wanted to strangle and get rid of him; to see him stretched out before her, beaten once and for all. For a moment they struggled together in silence, breathing in gasps, their limbs cracking with the strain. It was no longer a game: there was a cold air of murder about them. Colombel's breath began rattling in his throat. Afraid that someone might overhear them, she pushed him in a final, terrible effort. His temple struck the corner of the dressing table and he slumped to the floor.

Thérèse stood for a moment, getting back her breath. She looked into the glass, smoothed back her hair, and patted the creases out of her skirt, deliberately ignoring her vanquished opponent. Then she prodded him with her foot. When he did not move, she bent over him, a chill prickling at the nape of her neck. She saw Colombel's wax-white face, his glassy eyes and twisted mouth. His right temple was smashed in by the corner of the table. Colombel was dead.

She straightened up, frozen with horror, and spoke aloud in the silence.

'Dead! So now he's dead.'

The sudden realization of what had happened filled her with searing anguish. For a second, she had certainly wanted to kill him. But it was merely a stupid angry thought. You always want to kill when you fight, but you don't, because having bodies around is too awkward. No, she was not guilty, because she had not intended to kill him. And to think that he was lying dead in her room!

She went on talking brokenly to herself.

'It's done now. He's dead and he won't leave here of his own accord.'

After the paralyzing stupor of the first few moments, a feverish feeling coursed like a flame through her whole body. A dead man was lying in her bedroom. She could never explain how he came to be there, with his feet bare, in his shirt sleeves, and with a hole in his temple. She was in a desperate fix.

Thérèse bent and looked at the wound. As she did so she froze with terror. She could hear Françoise, Colombel's mother, in the corridor. And there were other noises in the house, footsteps and voices and the preparations for the reception to be held that very evening. Any minute now someone might call her or come looking for her. The lover she had killed seemed to have reversed their roles and was now weighing her down with their guilt.

Her head reeled and she got up and began walking round and round her room. She sought some corner in which to hide the corpse sprawling across her very future. She peered under the furniture and probed into corners, trembling with fury at her own helplessness. No, there was not a single corner; the alcove was not deep enough, the wardrobes were too shallow—nothing in the whole room was of any use as a hiding place. Yet it was there that they had concealed their kisses! He used to come in with his quiet, catlike, and viciously stealthy step and leave in the same way. She would never have imagined that he could have become so heavy.

Thérèse stamped and raged around her room with the vibrant anger of a hunted animal, and then she had an inspiration. Suppose she threw Colombel out the window? But then he would be found and they would guess from which window he had fallen. Nevertheless, she had crossed to the window and raised the curtain to look out and suddenly she saw the young man who lived opposite, that idiot who played the flute, leaning on his window sill with a hangdog air. His pale face was well-known to her, since he was always staring at her window. She was tired of that face and its cringing devotion to her. She stopped when she saw Julien, so humble and lovesick. A smile lit her pale face. There lay her salvation. That fool across the way loved her with the passion of a chained dog and would obey her, even to the extent of committing a crime. She had never felt any love toward him because he was too gentle, but she would make love to him and buy his eternal devotion with the gift of her body if he would share with her the blood of her crime. Her tongue flicked over her scarlet lips as if tasting a love spiced with terror that, because it was untasted, attracted her the more.

She snatched up Colombel's body like a bundle of wash and carried it to her bed. Then, opening her window, she blew kisses to Julien.

IV

Julien was plunged into a nightmare. When he recognized Colombel on the bed he was not surprised—he found it quite predictable and natural. Who but Colombel could have been lying there in the alcove, with his temple smashed in and his limbs sprawling in a position of hideous lewdness?

Thérèse had been talking to him for a long time. At first, he did not hear what she was saying and the words she spoke penetrated his stupor only as a confused noise. Then he realized that she was giving him orders and he made an effort to listen to her. He was to stay in the room until midnight, when the house would be dark and the guests gone. Because of the party her mother was giving, it was out of the question to do anything earlier, but the evening's entertainment had its advantages because it meant that everyone was too busy to go up to Thérèse's room. When the right time came, Julien would have to hoist the body onto his back, carry it out of the house, and throw it into the Chanteclair at the end of the Rue Beau-Soleil. According to the calm plan outlined by Thérèse, nothing could be easier.

She stopped talking and, placing her hands on his shoulders, asked, 'Do you understand? It's agreed, isn't it?'

He shuddered.

'Yes, yes, anything you wish. I belong to you, body and soul.'

With a solemn expression, she leaned toward him and because he did not understand what she wanted of him, she said, 'Kiss me.'

Trembling, he kissed her on her cold forehead. Neither of them spoke.

Thérèse had drawn the bed curtains. She dropped into the armchair in the shadows to snatch a little rest. After standing for a moment, Julien also sat down. Françoise was no longer in the next room and only muffled sounds reached the quiet and gradually darkening room.

For nearly an hour nothing stirred. The throbbing in Julien's head prevented him from thinking clearly. He was in Thérèse's room and that filled him with bliss. Then, when he suddenly remembered there was a corpse behind the curtains that brushed against him, he thought he would faint. Had she loved that creature? How in God's name was it possible? He forgave her for having killed him, but what enraged him was the sight of Colombel's bare feet lying among the lace-edged bed linen. How pleased he would be to chuck him from the bridge into that dark, deep part of the Chanteclair that he knew so well. Once they were rid of him, they could set about making love. Then, at the thought of the delight of which he would not dared to have dreamed that morning, he imagined himself on the bed instead of that lolling corpse, and the idea of the coldness of that place which he would take filled him with loathing.

Thérèse sat motionless in her deep armchair. All Julien could see of her was the outline of her hair against the pale light of the window. She sat there with her face in her hands and he could only guess at the cause of her exhaustion. Was it just physical relaxation after the terrible ordeal through which she had just gone? Was it crushing remorse, an emptiness left by her lover who was now sleeping his last sleep? Was she calmly working out the details of her plan of salvation, or was she hiding in the shadows the ravages that fear had left on her face? He had no way of telling.

In the silence the clock struck. Thérèse rose slowly to her feet and lit the candles on her dressing table, seeming as calm, poised, and strong as usual. She appeared to have forgotten about the body sprawling behind the pink silk curtains and went about the room with the unhurried step of a girl completely at ease in her own room. As she let her hair down she said, without turning around, 'I have to dress this evening. If anyone comes in you'll hide, won't you?'

He sat there, looking at her. She already treated him like a lover, as if the blood-stained complicity between them had created the understanding of a long love affair.

She dressed her hair, her hand raised above her head. He shivered as he watched her, finding her so desirable, with her bare back turned toward him, her elbows moving slowly, her slender hands twisting curls upon her fingers. Did she wish to win him over completely, show him the woman who would be his if he did what she wanted?

When she had put on her shoes, there was a sound outside the door.

'Hide in the alcove,' she said in a low voice.

Swiftly she threw over Colombel's stiff body the underclothes she had just removed, still warm and scented by her body.

Françoise came in and said, 'They're waiting for you, mademoiselle.'

'I'm just coming, Françoise dear,' Thérèse replied calmly. 'Give me a hand with my dress, will you?'

Through a chink in the curtains, Julien could see the two women and he trembled at Thérèse's audacity. His teeth chattered so much that he took his lower jaw in his hand so that he would not be overheard. Beside him, one of Colombel's bare feet peeped out from under a petticoat. Suppose Françoise had opened the curtains and bumped into her son's naked foot!

'Be careful,' said Thérèse, 'you'll tear the flowers off.'

There was not a tremor in her voice. She was smiling, a girl pleased to be going to a dance. Her frock was of white silk printed with wild roses, the white petals of which had a touch of crimson in the center. Standing in the middle of the room, she looked like a bouquet of flowers, white and virginal. Her bare arms and neck blended with the whiteness of her dress.

'Oh, how lovely you look, how lovely,' repeated Françoise with deep satisfaction. 'One moment, you don't have your garland.'

She seemed to be looking for it and stretched out a hand to the curtains as though about to search on the bed. Julien almost cried out aloud in terror. But Thérèse said unhurriedly, smiling at her reflection in the mirror, 'It's over there on my dressing table. Give it to me. No, don't touch my bed; all my clothes are there and you'll muddle them up.'

Françoise helped her to place the garland of wild roses on her head, like a crown, with one end trailing onto her neck. Thérèse stood for a moment looking at herself with satisfaction.

Then she was ready and drew on her gloves.

'Ah!' exclaimed Françoise. 'There's not a statue of the Virgin in church that looks as white and pure as you!'

The compliment made Thérèse smile again. She looked at herself once more in the glass and walked toward the door, saying, 'Come, let's go down. You may blow out the candles.'

In the sudden darkness, Julien heard the door close and the silken swish of Thérèse's dress along the corridor. He sat on the floor at the back of the alcove, not daring to go out. A deep blackness hung like a veil before his eyes, but he sensed the naked foot beside him that seemed to freeze the entire room. He had no idea how long he sat there, his thoughts weighing on his mind like a kind of drowsiness, when the door opened again. He recognized the sound of Thérèse's dress. She did not go up to him, but merely set something down on the dressing table and whispered, 'There, you've had no dinner. You must eat, you know.'

The silken sound faded away down the corridor again. Julien got up; he could no longer stay suffocating in the alcove with Colombel. The clock struck eight and there were still four hours to go. He tiptoed soundlessly across the room.

By the faint light of the starlit night, he could make out the dark shapes of the furniture. Some corners of the room were buried in darkness.

Only the looking glass cast a pale reflection, like that of old silver. He was not easily frightened, but in that somber room sweat ran down his face. All around him the dark shapes of the furniture seemed to move and take on menacing outlines. Three times he thought he heard sighs from the alcove. He halted in his tracks, terrified. Then, as he strained his ears, he heard gay sounds from below, a dance tune, the laughing murmur of a crowd. He closed his eyes and suddenly he was no longer in a dark pit. Bright lights blazed and he saw Thérèse, in a pure white dress, waltzing down a glittering room in the arms of her partner. The whole house echoed to the sound of merry music while he was there in that hideous place, alone and with chattering teeth. At one moment he started back in horror, thinking he had seen a light on a chair. When he plucked up courage to go over and see what it was, he found a white satin bodice. He took it in his hands, buried his face in the material softened by the young girl's breasts, and drugged himself with the smell of her.

There was such delight there that he wanted to forget everything. It was not a deathwatch he was keeping, but a love watch. He pressed his forehead against the windowpane and went over his love story. There, on the other side of the street, he could see his room with the windows still open. From there he had wooed Thérèse during long evenings of playing the flute that had confessed his love with the gentle voice of a shy lover, until she had been won over and smiled at him. The satin he held to his lips belonged to her, satin that had touched her skin and that she had left with him so he would not be impatient. His dream became so real that he left the window and ran to the door, thinking he had heard her.

The chill of the room struck and sobered him and then he remembered everything. Furiously, he made up his mind. He would return to her that very night. She was too beautiful and he loved her too much to wait. Where there is love and a crime has been committed, one must love with body-searing passion. Yes, he would come back, running and without losing a single minute, once the package had been cast in the river. Maddened by a sudden attack of nerves, he rolled his head in the bodice, biting the satin to choke his sobbing lust.

Ten o'clock struck. He listened, feeling he had been there for years, and waited in a daze. His hand touched the bread and fruit on the table and he ate standing up, ravenously and with a hunger he could not stay. He thought that food might give him strength, but once he had eaten, a terrible weariness overcame him. Night seemed to go on forever. From below the music rose louder, now and then the dancing shook the floor beneath his feet, and then carriages began to roll away from the house. His eyes were fixed on the door and he saw a kind of star of light shining through the keyhole. He did not even try to hide. If somebody came in, then that was that.

'No, thank you, Françoise,' said Thérèse, coming into the room, candle in hand, 'I can manage alone. Go to bed, you must be tired.'

She closed the door and locked it. Finger to lips and candlestick in hand, she stood still for a moment. Dancing had not brought the slightest color to her cheeks. She said nothing and, setting down the candle, sat facing Julien. For half an hour they waited, looking at each other.

The downstairs doors finished banging and the house was quiet. Thérèse's greatest worry was that Françoise's room was next door. The old woman moved around in her room for a moment and then her bed creaked as she retired for the night. For a long time she tossed in her bed as though unable to get to sleep, but at last her deep regular breathing could be heard through the wall.

Thérèse continued to stare seriously at Julien. She said only two words.

'Come on.'

They drew back the bed hangings and set about dressing little Colombel's corpse, already as stiff as a macabre puppet. When at last they finished, their foreheads ran with sweat.

'Come on,' she said again.

Without hesitation and in a single movement, Julien swung Colombel's body across his shoulders, as a butcher carries a calf. His great, bony frame was bent and Colombel's feet swung a yard from the floor.

'I'll lead the way,' whispered Thérèse quickly. 'I'll hold onto your coat and you just let yourself be guided by me. And go slowly.'

First they had to go through Françoise's room. That was the worst part of all. They had crossed it when one of the corpse's legs banged against a chair. The noise woke Françoise. They heard her raise her head from the pillow and mumble to herself. They stood, frozen to the floor, Thérèse near the door and he, weighed down by the body and terrified that the mother would discover them carrying her dead son to the river. It was a horrible moment. Then Françoise seemed to go to sleep again and they went out carefully into the corridor.

There another terror lay in wait for them. Thérèse's mother was still awake and a sliver of light came from her door, which was still ajar. They were too frightened to go either forward or backward. Julien felt that Colombel would slip from off his shoulders if they had to retrace their steps through Françoise's room. For nearly a quarter of an hour they stood stock still and

Thérèse found courage enough to hold up the body so that Julien should not tire. At last the light went out and they were able to get down to the ground floor. They were safe at last.

Thérèse opened the old unused door. When Julien found himself in the middle of the Place des Quatre Femmes, with his load on his back, he could see her standing at the top of the steps, her white arms and white evening dress gleaming. She was waiting for him to come back.

V

Julien was as strong as a bull. As a boy, he liked helping the woodsmen in the forest near his home and carried tree trunks on his young back. To him Colombel was no heavier than a feather; the skinny fellow was no more than a bird on his back. He scarcely felt him there and was suddenly filled with a wicked delight at the feeling that Colombel was so light, so thin, like nothing at all, in fact. No longer would he sneer at him as he passed beneath Julien's window when he played the flute, and his sarcastic remarks in the street were over forever. The thought that he carried a rival on his back, stiff and cold, gave Julien a shiver of satisfaction. He hitched the corpse up onto the nape of his neck, gritted his teeth, and walked faster.

The town was in darkness. Yet there was a light at Captain Pidoux's window in the Place des Quatre Femmes. The captain was probably out of sorts and the distorted shadow of his big-bellied form could be seen crossing and recrossing the room behind the curtains. Alarmed at this, Julien was slipping along in the shadow of the houses on the other side when a sudden cough froze his blood. He stopped in a doorway and recognized Madame Savournin, the lawyer's wife, sitting at her window, gazing at the stars and sighing to herself. This was a quirk of fate, because usually at this time the Place des Quatre Femmes was wrapped in slumber. Fortunately, Madame Savournin decided at last to return to the side of her husband, whose deep snoring reverberated through the open window into the street. When the window had been closed, Julien walked quickly across the square, keeping an eye on the undulating and distorted shadow of Captain Pidoux.

Once he got into the narrow alley of the Rue Beau-Soleil, he was less frightened. The houses leaned so close to one another and the cobbled slope was so crooked that the starlight did not reach into the bottom of the trenchlike street filled with a thick stream of shadow. Once there and in shelter, Julien was filled with a mad desire to run, and he set off at a mad gallop. It was both dangerous and stupid. He knew that, but he could not help himself, feeling behind him the starlit square of the Place des Quatre Femmes, with the windows of the lawyer's wife and the captain like two great watching eyes on his back. His shoes made such a clatter on the stones that he thought he was being followed. Suddenly he stopped. From the blonde widow's dining club, thirty yards down the Rue Beau-Soleil, came the voices of the officers gathered there. They were probably drinking a toast to one of their comrades whose promotion had just come through. Julien knew that he was lost if they came back along the street. There was no intersecting street down which he could escape and he would certainly have no time to retrace his steps. Holding his breath until he nearly choked, he listened to the tramp of boots and the clicking noise of scabbards. For a moment he could not tell if the sounds were coming his way or going in the opposite direction. Little by little, the noise died away. He waited for a moment and then went on his way on tiptoe. If he had had time to take his boots off he would have gone barefoot.

At last he reached the town gate. There was neither tollhouse nor sentry and he could go through freely. But the sudden spread of countryside as he came out of the Rue Beau-Soleil terrified him. The landscape was completely blue, a very pale blue. A country freshness was wafted to him and he had the feeling that a vast crowd was waiting for him and breathing into his face. They could see him, and a sudden clamor would root him to the spot.

But the bridge was there. He could see the white road, the parapets on either side, low and gray like granite seats, and he could hear the rippling of the Chanteclair between the tall reeds. At last he plucked up courage to walk on, bent almost double, avoiding the open spaces, afraid of being seen by the thousands of mute witnesses he imagined surrounded him. The most alarming stretch was on the bridge itself, for once he found himself standing there the whole town was spread out behind him like an amphitheater. He wanted to go to the end of the bridge to where he usually sat, swinging his legs and breathing the sweetness of the night air. In a deep pool the Chanteclair seemed to spread like a black, still cloth dimpled with little swirls thrown up by the racing whirlpool beneath. He had often amused himself by throwing stones in, to guess at the depth of water by the bubbles. With a final effort of will, he crossed the bridge.

Yes, that was the place. He recognized the stone, polished by the long hours he had sat there. He leaned over and looked down into the dimpled surface of the pool. This was the spot; he unloaded his burden onto the parapet. He could not resist having a last look at Colombel before throwing him into the water. The eyes of the whole town would not have stopped him. He stayed there for a moment, face to face with the corpse. The hole in Colombel's temple had turned black. Far away in the sleeping country-side the wheels of a cart groaned. Julien hurried about his task and, so as not to make too loud a splash, he raised the body once more and let it down slowly into the water, leaning over with it. Without Julien's knowing quite how it happened, the dead man's arms became locked around his neck and he began to fall, just saving himself by grabbing at a ledge. Colombel had wanted to take Julien with him.

When he sat alone once more on the parapet he was completely exhausted, his back bent and his legs hanging limp, as he had so often sat on returning from a long walk. He looked at the still surface of the water with its smiling ripples. One thing was certain: Colombel, although he was dead, had wanted to take him along with him. But it was all over now. Julien breathed deeply, inhaling the fresh smell of the fields. He looked along the silver shimmer of the river between the velvet shadows of the trees, and the country-side seemed to him like a promise of peace, a long rest in perfect and sheltered surroundings.

Then he remembered Thérèse. He was sure she was waiting for him. He could still see her in his mind's eye, standing at the top of the steps in front of that old moss-covered door. She was standing up straight, in her white silk dress with the crimson-centered wild roses. Perhaps she felt the cold. Then she would have gone up to her room to wait for him. She would have left the door ajar and lain down in her bed like a bride on her wedding night.

Ah, what delights awaited him! No woman had waited for him like that. In a few moments he would keep their tryst. But his legs were leaden and he was afraid of falling asleep. Was he a coward? To pull himself together, he thought of Thérèse changing her clothes. He imagined her arms raised above her head, her breasts thrust forward, her elbows and pale hands. He goaded himself with his memories—the smell of her body, her soft skin, the terrifying sensuality that had already intoxicated him in her room. Was he going to give up all that passion which had been offered to him, the foretaste of which still burned his lips? No, even if his legs refused to carry him, he would drag himself there on his knees.

But he had already lost the battle and his love was guttering out. His one desire was to sleep, to sleep forever. In his mind the picture of Thérèse faded and a black wall took its place. Now he would have been unable to lay even a finger on her shoulder without dying. His lust died amid a smell of corpses. Everything had become too impossible; the ceiling would have fallen in on them had he gone back to that room and held Thérèse to him.

To sleep and to sleep forevermore—that was the only thing worthwhile when there was no longer anything to wake up for. He would not go to the post office tomorrow, he would never play the flute again, he would no longer sit at his window. So why not sleep until the end of time? His life had come to an end and he could lie down and sleep. He looked again at the river, trying to see if Colombel were still there. Colombel had been very intelligent and he knew what he was doing when he tried to take Julien with him.

The surface of the pool spread below, dappled with the quick laughter of the whirlpool. There was a musical gentleness about the Chanteclair and the countryside lay in peace. Julien murmured Thérèse's name three times and then let himself fall, toppling over and over like a bundle before throwing up a great cloud of spray. And the Chanteclair went singing on its way between the reeds.

When the two bodies were found, it was assumed there had been a fight and a whole story was woven around it. It was thought that Julien had lain in wait for Colombel, to get back at him for the teasing he had suffered, and that he had thrown himself into the river after killing Colombel by battering in his temple with a stone.

Three months later, Mademoiselle Thérèse de Marsanne was married to young Count de Véteuil. Her wedding dress was white and her beautiful face radiated a calm and chaste pride.

ROUND TRIP

LUCIEN BÉRARD and Hortense Larivière had been married for exactly one week. For thirty years Hortense's mother, the Widow Larivière, had kept the fancy-goods shop in the Rue de la Chaussée d'Antin. Dried-out, vinegary, and tyrannical by nature, she had been unable to stop her daughter from marrying the only son of a neighboring ironmonger but she had every intention of keeping a close eye on the young couple. The shop had been given to Hortense as her dowry and the widow retained one room in the house for her own use. In fact, she still ran the business under the pretext of teaching the young couple how to do so.

It was August and very hot. Business was poor and Madame Larivière's temper was even shorter than usual. She never left Lucien and Hortense to themselves for an instant. Hadn't she surprised them one morning kissing at the back of the shop? And already married for a week, if you please! A fine way of carrying on and just the sort of thing that gets a shop a good name. She had never let Monsieur Larivière so much as lay a finger on her in the shop and it would never have entered his mind to try to do so. That was how they had built up their business.

Lucien did not as yet dare fly the flag of revolt openly so he blew kisses to Hortense behind his mother-in-law's back. One day he plucked up courage to say that the two families had agreed, before the wedding, to pay for a honeymoon.

Madame Larivière set her lips in a thin line and replied, 'All right, go for a walk in the Bois de Vincennes.'

The young couple looked at each other in dismay and Hortense decided that her mother's attitude was becoming thoroughly ridiculous. Even at night, she scarcely had a chance to be alone with her husband. At the slightest sound Madame Larivière would pad barefoot to the door of their room, knock, and ask if they were ill; and when they answered that they were in the best of health she told them, 'Well, you ought to be asleep or you'll be nodding over the counter again tomorrow.'

It had become unbearable. Lucien talked of tradesmen who went off on jaunts while their parents or a reliable assistant looked after their shops. The man who kept the glove shop at the corner of the Rue La Fayette had gone to Dieppe, the cutler in the Rue Saint-Nicolas had just left for Luchon, and the jeweler near the boulevard had taken his wife to Switzerland. Nowadays everybody who had a little money spent a month in the country.

'Yes, I know they do—and that's the way business goes to the dogs,' declared Madame Larivière. 'When my husband was alive, we used to go to the Bois de Vincennes on Easter Monday and we were none the worse for going out only once a year. Let me tell you something. Those globe-trotting habits are the surest way of losing trade. Mark my words, the business will go downhill.'

'But it was agreed that we should go away,' protested Hortense. 'Don't you remember, Maman, you promised?'

'Maybe I did—but that was before the wedding and a lot of silly things are said before weddings. Come on now, be sensible.'

To avoid a row, Lucien left the house but he would gladly have throttled his mother-in-law. Two hours later he came back in a totally different mood and spoke very mildly to the widow, the hint of a smile on his face.

That evening he asked Hortense, 'Have you ever been to Normandy?'

'You know perfectly well,' she replied, 'that I have never been farther than the Bois de Vincennes.'

Then came a bolt from the blue. Lucien's father, known to everyone in that part of Paris as Old Bérard, a man who enjoyed life and was also a shrewd businessman, invited himself to lunch. When coffee was served he said, 'I've brought a present for the children'—and brandished triumphantly a couple of railway tickets.

'What's that?' the widow asked in a choked voice.

'Two first-class tickets for a round trip to Normandy. There you are, my dears, a month in the open air for you. You'll come back with roses in your cheeks.'

This completely took the wind out of Madame Larivière's sails. She would have liked to protest but wanted at all costs to avoid a quarrel with Old Bérard, because he always had the last word. To cap it all, Bérard talked about whisking the young couple off to the station right away. He would not let them out of his sight until they were safely on the train.

'That's right, take my daughter away from me,' said the widow in a blind rage. 'I'd rather have it that way; then they won't be able to go kissing all over the shop and I can keep our good name.'

So Hortense and Lucien arrived at the Gare Saint-Lazare, escorted by Lucien's father, who had given them just time enough to toss a few clothes into a suitcase before they left home. He gave them both smacking kisses on their cheeks and told them to have a good look at everything so that they could tell him all about it when they came home. He'd look forward to that, he said.

Lucien and Hortense hurried down the corridor of the train to try and find an empty compartment. They found one and were just settling in nicely and looking forward to a long talk when, to their dismay, a man climbed in, sat down, and began staring sternly at them from behind his spectacles. As the train moved out of the station, Hortense, bitterly disappointed at this intrusion, turned to the window and pretended to watch the countryside—but she could not even see the trees for the tears in her eyes.

Lucien tried to think up some ingenious way of getting rid of the old man, but the only solutions that came to mind were far too violent to be carried out. At first he hoped that their fellow passenger might get out at Mantes or Vernon, but unfortunately he was going right through to Le Havre. So, in exasperation, Lucien decided to hold Hortense's hand; they were married, after all. The old man's expression became even more stern and it was so obvious that he thoroughly disapproved of this display of feeling in public that Hortense, blushing, withdrew her hand from her husband's. The rest of the journey was spent in silence. Fortunately, they soon reached Rouen.

Before leaving Paris, Lucien had bought himself a guidebook and they went to one of the hotels he had looked up in it. They were immediately pounced on by hotel porters and waiters and could barely get up courage to talk to each other under the stares of other guests in the dining room. When at last dinner came to an end, they went straight up to their room, but the walls were so thin that they could hear the slightest movement in the adjoining rooms and so neither dared stir in bed or even cough.

Next morning Lucien said, 'Let's look around the town and then leave as quickly as we can for Le Havre.'

They walked around all day, visiting the Cathedral and the Butter Tower, which got its name from the local tax on butter that contributed toward the cost of its construction. They looked at the palace of the bygone Dukes of Normandy, at disused churches turned into storehouses for fodder, at Saint Joan of Arc's Square, the museum, and even the cemetery. They did not miss a single historic building but walked from one to another as though fulfilling a duty. Hortense was bored to tears and so worn out that she fell asleep in the train next day.

A further annoyance awaited them at Le Havre. The beds in the hotel they stayed at were so narrow that they were put in a room with two single beds. Hortense saw a deliberate insult in this and began to weep. To console her, Lucien swore that they would stay in Le Havre just long enough to look around—and once more the mad rush began.

After Le Havre they stayed in turn in each place of importance listed in their itinerary. They saw Honfleur, Pont l'Evêque, Caen, Bayeux, Cherbourg—their minds reeling at the succession of streets and monuments. They muddled up churches and became bemused by the ever-changing cavalcade of sights that did not interest them in the slightest. Nowhere could they find a spot in which to kiss in peace out of range of inquisitive ears. They reached the stage where they no longer looked at anything, but carried out their itinerary to the letter like an unavoidable drudgery. One evening when they were in Cherbourg, Lucien let slip a remark that showed how serious the situation had become: 'I think I'd rather put up with your mother than do this.'

Next day they left for Granville. Lucien sat solemnly in his corner, glancing with a rather wild look in his eye at the fields unfolding like a fan on either side of the train. Suddenly, as the train stopped at a little station, the name of which he did not even catch, he exclaimed, 'Come on, dear, let's go out at once!'

'But this place isn't mentioned in the guide-book!' said Hortense in astonishment.

'Oh, that damned guidebook!' he shouted. 'You just wait and see what I do with it. Come on, quickly.'

'What about our luggage?'

But Hortense got out and the train pulled away, leaving just the two of them standing there in the middle of a sweet green isolation. The moment they walked out of the station, they were in the heart of the country. The only sounds were the singing of the birds in the trees and the ripple of a little stream through the valley. The first thing Lucien did was to chuck the guidebook into the middle of a pond. They were free at last!

A few hundred yards away, they came to a lonely inn where the landlady rented them a large white-washed room that was as gay as spring itself. The walls were three feet thick and, what is more, there were no other guests. Only the hens looked at them inquisitively.

'Our tickets are good for another week,' said Lucien, 'so we'll spend it here.'

And what a wonderful week that was! Each morning they set off along deserted footpaths running deep into the woods or up to the slopes of a hill, where they spent all day making love in the tall grass. Sometimes they wandered along the bank of the stream and Hortense, like a child playing truant from school, took off her shoes and stockings to paddle and gasped as Lucien suddenly kissed the nape of her neck. Their lack of clean clothes and luggage did not worry them, they were so thrilled to be alone and far away from everyone and everything. Hortense borrowed the landlady's underclothes and the coarse linen tickled her skin and made her giggle. At eight o'clock every evening, when the darkening and silent countryside no longer tempted them, they locked themselves in their cheerful bedroom. They particularly asked never to be awakened in the morning. Sometimes Lucien went down in his slippers and carried upstairs a breakfast of chops and eggs, allowing nobody but himself to go into their room. Those were delicious meals, eaten on the edge of the bed and spun out by kisses as numerous as the mouthfuls of bread.

When their last day came, they were surprised and sad that their stay had come to an end so quickly. They left without even attempting to find out the name of the place in which they had learned to love each other. At least they had enjoyed a quarter of their honeymoon. They only caught up with their luggage in Paris.

They got into a muddle when Old Bérard started asking questions about the trip. They had seen the sea at Caen and they shifted the Butter Tower to Le Havre.

'But you haven't even mentioned Cherbourg and the arsenal,' said the ironmonger.

'Oh, it's only a small arsenal,' replied Lucien blandly. 'And there aren't any trees.'

At this point Madame Larivière, as grim as

ever, shrugged her shoulders and muttered, 'Travel's nothing but a waste of time. They don't even remember the monuments of historical interest. Enough of that nonsense—get back to the counter, Hortense.'

WINKLES FOR MONSIEUR CHABRE

I

THE bane of Monsieur Chabre's life was his
wife's failure to bear him a child. He had married Estelle Catinot, of the Desvignes and Catinot
family, when she was a tall, beautiful blonde of
eighteen, and for four years he had been waiting anxiously, not only worried but wounded
by the apparent uselessness of his efforts to beget
an heir.

Monsieur Chabre had made a lot of money
as a grain merchant before retiring. He had
led the usual chaste life of a solid middle-class
businessman whose eyes had been firmly fixed
on his goal of making a million francs. Now, at
forty-five, he plodded around in the heavy-
footed way of a man already weighed down by
the years. His pallid face was lined by money-
making worries and was as flat as a flagstone.
Having made a fortune on which to retire, he
was almost in despair at finding it more difficult
to become a father than to become rich.

Madame Chabre was a delightful girl of
twenty-two with a complexion like a ripe peach
and hair that had the glint of sunshine and

reached to her shoulders. Her eyes were of that blue-green color of still waters in which it is hard to see anything. When her husband complained about their lack of children, she drew herself up to display her slender waist, her ample hips and bosom, and answered him with a hint of a smile on her lips, 'Is it my fault?'

It should be said at once that in their family circle Madame Chabre was considered a girl of impeccable behavior and untouched by gossip. She was, in fact, a devoted wife who had been raised in the good middle-class virtues by a strict mother. Nonetheless, any husband other than the retired grain merchant would have been uneasy about her habit of dilating her nostrils in a nervous gesture now and then.

Monsieur Chabre had often talked confidentially with his family doctor, Guiraud, a big, intelligent, amiable man who explained that science still had a lot to learn. You could not, for God's sake, plant a child as easily as you plant an oak tree. But Dr. Guiraud never wished a patient to give up hope, so he told Monsieur Chabre that he would give very careful thought to his problem.

One July morning, he gave Monsieur Chabre a bit of advice.

'You ought to take up swimming, my dear sir. I can assure you that it is most beneficial. Furthermore, I prescribe for you a strict diet of shellfish. Plenty of shellfish and nothing but shellfish.'

Hope sprang anew in the breast of Monsieur Chabre and he inquired, with considerable excitement, 'Shellfish, Doctor? Do you really mean to say that shellfish—?'

'Precisely. It has been proved that as a diet it is most beneficial. No, listen carefully. Every day you must eat oysters, mussels, clams, sea urchins, winkles—yes, lobsters and crawfish too.'

As Dr. Guiraud was leaving, he turned at the door and added lightly, 'But don't go and bury yourself somewhere. Madame Chabre is young and she needs a bit of distraction. The air at Trouville is first class. I'd go there if I were you.'

Three days later, Monsieur and Madame Chabre duly left for the seashore. After thinking about it, Monsieur Chabre had decided that they need not go to Trouville, where it was certainly expensive. You can eat shellfish pretty well anywhere at the seashore and, what is more, it would be cheaper and more plentiful in some small and secluded spot on the coast. And as for amusements—well, there was always too much of that around, and it was not exactly for pleasure that the Chabres were going away.

One of Monsieur Chabre's friends recommended a little place called Pouliguen near Saint-Nazaire. After twelve hours on the train, a day in Saint-Nazaire bored Madame Chabre to tears. It was a new town with bare, straight streets, some still half built and bustling with workmen. The Chabres looked around the port, then strolled through the streets, where the shops were still hesitating between remaining poky village groceries or becoming large and resplendent city-style stores.

When they reached Pouliguen, the Chabres found that there was not a single villa to let. All the little wood and plaster houses, painted in gaudy colors like fairground huts and dotted around the bay, were already occupied by English visitors and the families of rich businessmen from Nantes. In any case, Estelle made a face when she saw the architectural styles in which full rein had been given to the imagination of middle-class artists.

They were advised to go on to Guérande and spend the night there. It was a Sunday and when they arrived around noon, Monsieur Chabre immediately fell under the spell of the place although his nature was by no means that of a poet. He was dumfounded by the sight of Guérande—that showpiece of medieval architecture within its encircling wall of fortifications, its deep and dark doorways, and its overhanging parapets. Estelle gazed at the silent town, girt by tall trees and walks, and in the still depths of her eyes was a smiling dreaminess. Their carriage rattled on its way, the horse trotted through a gateway, and the wheels skidded over the sharp stones of the narrow, paved streets. Husband and wife had not exchanged a single word until Monsieur Chabre said, 'This is the back of beyond. The villages around Paris are much better built than this place.'

As they stepped out of their carriage in front of the Hôtel du Commerce in the center of the town, the congregation was coming out from morning Mass at the church next door. Estelle took a few steps around the square while her husband supervised the unloading of their baggage. She was most interested by the sight of the faithful parading by, many of them in regional costume. Some of the men wore white blouses and baggy trousers—these were the marsh dwellers from the great salt marsh that stretches between Guérande and Le Croisic. Quite distinct from them were local smallholders in short linen jackets and wide-brimmed hats. But what fascinated Estelle most of all were the clothes worn by a young girl whose hair was drawn back tightly. She wore a red blouse with wide turned-back sleeves, the bodice embroidered with brightly colored silk flowers. Her three skirts of blue linen, each tightly pleated and worn one over the other, were held by a belt worked in gold and silver thread. Over her skirts was tied an apron of orange silk, short enough to show her red woolen stockings and tiny yellow slippers.

'Well, I never,' said Monsieur Chabre, coming up behind his wife. 'You have to come to Brittany to see a carnival like that.'

Estelle did not answer. Just at that moment a tall young man of about twenty had come out of the church with an old woman on his arm. His skin was very white, his expression proud, and his hair was blond with a reddish tinge. His broad shoulders and muscular limbs made him seem a giant and yet, at the same time, there was something fine-drawn and almost delicate about him, and his face was pink and white as a girl's and without a trace of beard on the cheeks. As Estelle was staring at him, astonished by his powerful build and handsome face, the boy turned, looked at her for a second, and blushed.

'Well, there is at least one who looks human,' muttered Monsieur Chabre. 'Make a good infantryman, that fellow.'

'That's Monsieur Hector,' said a maid from the hotel who had overheard him. 'The lady with him is his mother, Madame de Plougastel. He's such a nice, quiet boy.'

During lunch at the hotel the Chabres were treated to a lively conversation. The commissioner for mortgages, who took all his meals there, boasted about the patriarchal way of life at Guérande. He also bragged of the exemplary behaviour of the young people. According to him, the chastity of the local people was guarded by their religious upbringing. He gave examples and quoted specific cases in support of his theme. But a commercial traveler, who had arrived that morning with his bags full of fake jewelry, sneered at his point of view and told how he had noticed, on his way into town, plenty of girls and boys kissing behind the hedges. He'd give his eyes to see, he said, some of these local boys' behavior if a few easy women were set down among them. He ended up by joking about religion, laughing at priests, and making fun of nuns, to such an extent that the commissioner for mortgages threw down his napkin and stalked out of the dining room, choking with rage.

The Chabres had not uttered a single word during the whole meal. Monsieur Chabre was furious about the subjects discussed in front of his wife, but Estelle had remained calm and smiling throughout, as if she had not understood what it was all about.

They spent the afternoon looking round Guérande. It was deliciously cool in the Church of Saint Aubin and they strolled around, gazing up at the vaulted roof where the tops of the columns splayed like rockets. They stopped and looked at the bizarre sculptures on the capitals of the columns—executioners sawing their victims in half, or roasting them over grids while keeping the fire going at the same time with enormous bellows. After that, they walked up and down the five or six streets of the town and Monsieur Chabre repeated his opinion that it was a back-of-beyond place without a glimmer of trade—a place surviving from the Middle Ages, like a lot of others that had already been torn down. The empty streets were lined with gabled houses leaning against one another like tired old women. The pointed roofs, the slate-covered corner turrets, the dormer windows, the outlines of carvings worn away by time, made some of the quiet corners seem like museums sleeping in the sun. Since her marriage, Estelle had read a number of books and she looked dreamily around and remembered Walter Scott's novels.

But once the Chabres had walked out of the town to look at it from the outside, they agreed that it was really rather enchanting. The solid granite walls, gilded by the sunlight, had remained unchanged and unbroken since the day they were built. Now nothing but trailing ivy and honeysuckle dropped from the machicolated ramparts. Shrubs had taken root on the towers and golden broom and flame wallflowers splashed in colored patches against the clear sky. All around the town were elm-shaded promenades, green with grass. It was like walking on a carpet beside the old moats that in some places had fallen in and in others remained as stagnant ponds whose weedy waters cast back weird reflections. The trunks of silver birches shone against the walls on which grew green tufts of plants. Between the trees, shafts of sunlight played on mysterious corners and postern gateways where only the frogs leaped swiftly through the silence of dead centuries.

'I've counted ten towers!' exclaimed Monsieur Chabre when they got back to the point from which they had started.

He had been struck most of all by the four deep and narrow town gates through which only a single carriage could pass at one time. Wasn't it ridiculous to stay walled up like that in the nineteenth century? If it were up to him, he would have pulled down those gatehouses that were forts in themselves, with their arrow slits and thick walls. A couple of six-story houses could have been put up in place of each gate.

'And that's without counting all the building material you could get out of the ramparts,' he added.

As they walked along the Mall, a great raised walk extending through a quarter of a circle from the east gate to the south gate, Estelle looked thoughtfully out at the horizon that stretched for mile upon mile beyond the roofs of the town. In the foreground was a line of rich natural vegetation, pines bent by the winds from the sea, tangled undergrowth, and thick dark bushes. Beyond that was the desolate expanse of the salt marshes, a wide and bare flatness with mirrors of square pools and the whiteness of small heaps of salt gleaming against the gray backdrop of the sands. And beyond that again, reaching to the limit of the sky, was the blue spread of the ocean, upon which three sails shone like white swallows.

'Look, there's the young fellow we saw this morning,' said Monsieur Chabre suddenly. 'Don't you think he's rather like the youngest Larivière boy? He'd look like his twin if only he had a hump on his back.'

Estelle turned around slowly but Hector, standing at the edge of the Mall, was also completely wrapped up in the distant prospect of the sea and did not seem to realize that he was being looked at. So Estelle started walking again, leaning on her long furled parasol. She had not taken more than a dozen steps when the parasol worked loose and fell to the ground and the Chabres heard a voice shouting, 'Madame! Madame!' Hector had retrieved it.

'Thank you very much, Monsieur,' said Estelle, with her slow smile.

He was indeed such a nice quiet young man that Monsieur Chabre took to him at once and told him about the trouble he was having in finding a good seaside place in which to stay. He even went so far as to ask the young man's advice.

Hector, who was very shy, stammered, 'I don't

think you'll find what you're looking for at either Croisic or Batz,'—and pointed to the church towers of these places on the horizon. 'I'd advise you to go to Piriac . . .'—and he went on to tell them how to get there. It was about seven and a half miles from Guérande and he had an uncle who lived nearby. In reply to a question put by Monsieur Chabre, he said he could vouch for the large number of shellfish to be had there.

Estelle, meanwhile, was prodding the short grass with the tip of her parasol. The young man did not look in her direction, as if he were embarrassed by her presence.

'Guérande is a very pretty town, Monsieur,' she said at last in her lilting voice.

'Oh . . . ah, yes—very pretty,' stammered Hector, staring fervently at her for a brief moment.

II

One morning, three days after the Chabres had moved to Piriac, Monsieur Chabre was standing at the end of the jetty that sheltered the little port. He was placidly watching over Estelle, who was taking her daily swim. She was floating on her back in the water. The sun was already high and Monsieur Chabre, who was attired with the utmost correctness—that is to say, in a black morning coat and trilby—was sheltering himself from the heat under a big tourist-type umbrella with a green lining.

'What's it like?' he asked, so as to give an appearance of interest in his wife's swimming.

'Very warm,' said Estelle, rolling over onto her stomach.

Monsieur Chabre never ventured into the sea. He was terrified of water but passed it off by saying untruthfully, that his doctors warned him strictly against swimming. If a wave broke on the shore and came anywhere near the soles of his shoes, he would spring back with a shudder, as though he had come face to face with a wild beast baring its fangs. Anyway, to go near the water would have disturbed his ideas of correct dress and he considered swimming both insanitary and improper.

'Oh, so the water's warm, is it?' he repeated, beginning to wilt in the heat and starting to get drowsy, planted there on his tiny jetty.

Estelle did not answer but started swimming, splashing about and doing a dog paddle. With boyish toughness she would stay in the sea for hours at a time. This dismayed her husband, since he thought it was only right and proper to wait for her on the shore. Estelle had found just the kind of swimming she liked at Piriac. She had no time for those gently-shelving beaches where you had to walk and walk before the water came up to your waist. She liked to go to the edge of the jetty wrapped in her white woolen bathrobe, let it drop to her feet, and dive in. She insisted that she needed eighteen feet of water so as not to hit the rocks at the bottom. Her one-piece bathing suit accentuated her height and the blue belt she wore showed to advantage her waist and hips, which were perfectly proportioned. Once in the water, her hair tucked under the cap from which a few strands escaped, she looked like a pale blue fish with the pink and intriguing face of a woman.

Monsieur Chabre had been sitting there in the blazing sunshine for a quarter of an hour. He had looked at his watch three times already and he eventually said, a trifle nervously, 'You're staying in a long time, dear. I think you ought to come out now. It's too tiring for you to be in the water too long.'

'But I just got in!' his young wife shouted back. 'And it's wonderfully warm, just like bathing in milk.'

Then she added, rolling over to float on her back again, 'If you're getting bored, why don't you go? There's no need for you to stay.'

Monsieur Chabre shook his head and replied that accidents can happen in a split second. Estelle smiled to herself at the thought of how much use her husband would be should she get a cramp. But suddenly she stared out to sea, beyond the jetty into the bay that lay to the left of the village.

'Look there,' she called, 'what's that? I'll go and see.'

And she swam off quickly with long, regular strokes.

'Estelle! Estelle!' Monsieur Chabre shouted after her, 'Don't go any farther. You know how I hate your taking risks like that.'

But he had to resign himself to staying there, since Estelle had not paid the slightest attention. He stood on tiptoe to watch the white patch on the water that was his wife's bathing cap and shifted his umbrella from one hand to the other as it became more and more stifling in its shadow.

'I wonder what it is she's seen?' he muttered to himself. 'Ah, yes, there *is* something floating out there, some kind of rubbish—seaweed or something like that, or an empty barrel. No, it can't be that because it's moving.'

Then he suddenly realized what it was. A man swimming!

In the meantime Estelle, having swum some distance, had quickly seen it was a man and stopped swimming straight for him in case she might appear indiscreet. And yet, with a sort of coquettish pleasure in showing off her strength, she did not turn back toward the jetty but went on toward the open sea. She swam calmly on without giving any sign of having seen the other swimmer. He, however, was getting nearer and nearer to her, as though carried by a current. When Estelle turned to swim back toward the jetty, they met—as if entirely by chance.

'I trust you are well, Madame?' the swimmer inquired with exquisite politeness.

'Oh, it's you, Monsieur!' Estelle exclaimed brightly, adding with a short laugh, 'So we meet again!'

It was young Hector de Plougastel—shy as ever and muscular and pink in the water. For a few moments they swam side by side without a word and keeping a decent distance between them. They had to raise their voices in order to hear each other. Estelle thought she should be polite and said, 'Thank you very much for having recommended Piriac to us. My husband is delighted with the place.'

'Is that your husband over there on the jetty, all alone?' asked Hector.

'Yes, Monsieur,' she replied.

And they lapsed into silence again as they looked toward Monsieur Chabre who, at that distance, seemed no larger than an insect perched above the surface of the sea. But Monsieur Chabre was very curious to know what was going on and he stood on tip-toe, craning his neck and wondering who his wife could have met way out at sea like that. There was no doubt she was talking to a man, because he could see their heads turning toward each other. It must be one of their Paris friends. He racked his brains but he could not think of anyone they knew who would be as adventurous as that. While he was waiting for them to reach the shore, he twirled his umbrella round and round—just to have something to do.

'You see,' Hector was explaining to beautiful Madame Chabre, 'I'm spending a few days with my uncle, who has a château down the coast over there. I come here every day for a swim; I go as far as the jetty and then I swim back. In all it's a mile and a half and it's good exercise. But, Madame, you are very brave. I have never met a lady who is as fearless in the water as you are.'

'Oh,' said Estelle, 'I started swimming when I was very small so I'm completely at home in the water. In fact the sea and I are old friends.'

Because they did not like shouting at each other as they talked, they came nearer and nearer. The sea was as calm as a sheet of silk in the heat of the morning. There were patches of satin spread out, then crisscross bands of rumpled cloth, alternately creasing and smoothing as they carried the ripple of currents.

Once Estelle and Hector were closer together, their conversation took a more friendly turn. First they agreed that it was a beautiful day and then Hector pointed out to Estelle the outstanding features of the coast. That village a mile beyond Piriac was called Port-aux-Loups and opposite it was Moribihan, with its white cliffs standing out as clear as a water color. In the other direction and out to sea was the island of Dumet, a gray shape in the middle of the blue sea. When Hector pointed out these landmarks, Estelle stopped swimming for a moment to look in the direction he was pointing. She found it fascinating to see, from the level of the water, those distant parts of the coast in a limpid infinity of distance. When she turned again toward the sun, the light was blinding and the sea seemed to turn into a kind of limitless Sahara, with the sunshine shimmering on immense stretches of bleached sand.

'How lovely it is, how lovely,' she murmured.

She turned on her back again to rest and lay motionless, with her hands crossed on her breast and her head lying back in surrender to the sea. Her pale legs and arms floated motionless and effortlessly.

'Were you born at Guérande, Monsieur?' she asked.

So as to make conversation easier, Hector also turned on his back.

'Yes, Madame,' he replied, 'and I have only been away once and that was just to Nantes.'

He went on to tell Estelle all about his upbringing, how he had never left his mother's side and how she was a strict Catholic who observed the traditions of the old nobility. Hector's tutor was a priest who had taught him along the lines of a Catholic College curriculum, with some embroidering on the mysteries of faith and points of heraldry. Hector had learned riding, fencing, and all kinds of athletic pursuits. Apart from these attributes, there was a kind of virgin innocence about him: he took Communion once a week, never read novels, and was intended at twenty-one as a husband for one of his cousins—an ugly one.

'You're barely twenty, then!' Estelle exclaimed, with a glance of astonishment at the boy colossus at her side.

A maternal feeling was aroused in her for this

interesting flower of the tough Breton race. But as they floated side by side on their backs, looking up into the transparent sky without a thought about where the land lay, they were carried closer together and bumped gently into each other.

'Oh, I'm so sorry,' he said.

He dived once more and surfaced again about twelve feet from Estelle, who had started swimming again and was laughing.

'We just collided!' she shouted.

Hector blushed deeply and swam close to her, watching her out of the corner of his eye. How delightful she was, with her dimpled chin in the water and drops sparkling on the blonde strands of hair that escaped from her cap, and trickled to glisten like pearls on her cheeks. How wonderful it was to watch her pretty, girlish face gliding silently through the water, to leave nothing in its wake but a silver thread in the sea.

Hector blushed even deeper when he realized that Estelle knew he was looking at her and was amused by the expression on his face.

'Your husband looks as if he's getting impatient,' he said, to get the conversation going again.

'Oh no,' she replied calmly, 'he's used to waiting for me when I go swimming.'

But Monsieur Chabre was in fact getting fidgety. He took four paces in one direction, turned and paced back again, twirling his umbrella more and more quickly in the hope of fanning a little cool air onto himself. His wife's long talk with the unknown swimmer surprised him.

It suddenly occurred to Estelle that Monsieur Chabre might not have recognized Hector.

'I'll call out to him that I've met you,' she said.

As soon as she was within hailing distance of the jetty, she shouted to her husband, 'You know who I'm with, dear—the gentleman from Guérande who was so helpful.'

'Ah, splendid, splendid!' Monsieur Chabre shouted back—and raised his hat.

'Is the water warm, Monsieur?' he inquired politely.

'Very warm indeed, Monsieur,' Hector replied.

Estelle continued her swim under her husband's supervision. Monsieur Chabre dared not complain, although his feet were starting to roast on the scorching stone. The water was crystal clear off the end of the jetty and the bed could be seen clearly, thirteen feet down, with its fine sand, a few scattered pebbles, and wispy seaweed waving upright in the water like long hair. These clear depths enchanted Estelle and she swam slowly so as not to ruffle the surface, putting her face into the water to look down at the pebbles in the mysterious sea bed below her. The delicate seaweed made her shiver slightly as she felt it brush against her. Thick patches, like living sheets of green, rolled in the tide. There were small torn leaves that waved like crabs' claws, and thick stalks that nestled between the rocks, and others that were long and supple and slender as snakes. Estelle gave a little cry as she made each new discovery.

'Oh, look at that big stone! You'd think it was moving! There's something like a real tree with branches! There's a fish—oh, look how quickly it swims.'

Then she suddenly said, 'Whatever is that? It looks like a bride's bouquet! I never knew there were brides' bouquets in the sea! They're exactly like white flowers, they're so pretty, they're really lovely.'

Hector dived to the sea bed and came up with a bunch of pale seaweed in his hand that drooped and wilted the moment it left the water.

'Thank you very much,' said Estelle. 'You really shouldn't have gone to all that trouble. Catch, dear, and keep it for me until I come out of the water.'

She tossed the handful of seaweed to Monsieur Chabre's feet. The young woman and the young man swam side by side again for a few moments, raising a boiling spray on the surface of the sea, shooting jerkily through the water with powerful strokes. Then, quite suddenly, they changed their style and glided gently through the water, touching it into widening circles that spread and trembled before vanishing. This floating in the same ripples brought a kind of tacit and sensual closeness to them. Hector tried to follow through the watery furrow that closed on Estelle's body as though he sought to capture the very place and warmth in which she had been. All around them the sea was calm and of a blue so pale that it held a tinge of pink.

'You'll catch cold, my dear,' called Monsieur Chabre, with beads of sweat coursing down his face.

'I'm just coming out, dear,' she answered.

With the help of a chain, she quickly hauled herself up the slope of the jetty. Hector must have noticed her climb out of the water, but when he looked up as the drops of water splashed down from her, she was already standing on the quayside, tightly wrapped in her bathrobe. Hector looked so surprised and disappointed that she could not help smiling at the expression on his face, although she was shivering a little. She shivered—knowing how charming she looked, standing there, tall and trembling, silhouetted against the sky.

Hector said that he had to go.

'We look forward to seeing you again, Monsieur,' said Monsieur Chabre.

Estelle, as she ran over the stones of the jetty,

watched Hector's head as he swam back across the bay, while Monsieur Chabre walked solemnly behind her, holding at arm's length the seaweed that Hector had gathered, to avoid staining his clothes with sea water.

III

The Chabres had rented the first floor of a large house at Piriac and their windows faced the sea. There were only a few ordinary bars and taverns in the village so they had to hire a local woman to cook for them. She produced some strange dishes—roasts turned to charcoal and sauces of such alarming shades that Estelle took one look at them and decided to stick to bread. But, as Monsieur Chabre pointed out, they had not gone there for the pleasures of the table. In any case, he practically never touched either the roasts or the sauces but applied himself to his shellfish, morning and evening, with the single-mindedness of a man taking his medicine. The trouble was that he loathed these unknown and oddly shaped creatures. Having been raised on very plain food—tasteless and watery, for the most part—he still had a childish sweet tooth. Full of salt and speckled with pepper, the shellfish burned his mouth and the taste of it was so strange and unexpectedly strong that it was all he could do not to make a face as he swallowed it. But he was so stubbornly bent on becoming a father that he would have eaten the shells too if necessary.

'You're not eating anything, dear,' he often told Estelle.

To obtain the desired results, she ought to eat as much as he, said Monsieur Chabre. This led to argument. Estelle maintained that Dr. Guiraud had said nothing about her, but Monsieur Chabre replied that it was logical that they should both undergo the same treatment. At this Estelle stared pointedly at her husband's pudgy plumpness and a slight smile brought out the dimple in her chin. But she said nothing, because she disliked hurting anyone's feelings. She even ate a dozen oysters at every meal after they discovered an oyster bed. It was not that she thought she needed oysters but because she happened to be very fond of them.

Life at Piriac was one of drowsy monotony. Only three families went to the beach—those of a wholesale grocer from Nantes; a retired Guérande lawyer, who was both deaf and stupid; and the third from Angers, who spent all day fishing, standing up to their waists in water. They were all very quiet and social intercourse never got beyond exchanging the time of day. The most exciting sight on the empty quayside was a couple of dogs having a fight.

Estelle was accustomed to the bustle of Paris and would have been bored to tears had it not been for Hector's daily visit. After he and Monsieur Chabre took a walk together along the shore, the older man became very friendly toward him. In a burst of confidence Monsieur Chabre told Hector why he and his wife had come to the seaside, choosing his words very carefully so as not to offend the young man's innocent ears. Having listened to Monsieur Chabre's explanation—given in scientific terms—as to why he ate so much shellfish, Hector, so flabbergasted that he forgot to blush, looked at him from head to foot without attempting to hide his surprise that a man should have to put himself on such a diet. Next day, however, he turned up with a small basket of clams for Monsieur Chabre, who gratefully accepted them.

Hector was a first-class fisherman and knew every rock in the bay. From that day on he never failed to bring shellfish when he visited the Chabres. Thanks to Hector, Monsieur Chabre ate superb mussels gathered by the young man at low tide, sea urchins that he opened and cleaned (pricking his fingers in doing so), limpets that he prized off the rocks with the point of his knife, and innumerable other kinds of shellfish with outlandish names that Hector himself had never tasted. Monsieur Chabre, because all this did not cost him a penny, was effusive in his thanks.

So now Hector always had an excuse for calling on them. Every time he arrived, basket in hand, he greeted Estelle in the same way: 'I've brought Monsieur Chabre his shellfish.'

And the two young people smiled at each other, their eyes sparkling, both amused by Monsieur Chabre's winkles and whelks.

Piriac seemed a charming place to Estelle from this time on. After her daily swim she went for a walk with Hector while her husband watched them from a distance because his legs ached and the young couple often went too fast for him.

Hector showed Estelle the bygone splendor of Piriac, the remains of carvings, the delicately sculpted foliage around doors and windows. What had been a town in the past was now nothing but an isolated village whose manure-strewn narrow streets were squeezed between blackened hovels. But the loneliness of the place was so quiet and gentle that Estelle skipped over the rubbish heaps and looked with interest at any old piece of wall and glanced with astonishment through the doors of cottages in which the confusion of poverty lay on the floors of beaten earth. Hector showed her the great fig trees that grew in the gardens, spreading their wide velvety leaves and their branches along the low walls. They walked into the narrowest alleys and leaned over the edges of wells and saw the reflection of their smiling faces, icily white in the clear water. Somewhere behind them, meanwhile, Monsieur Chabre digested his shellfish in the green calico shadow cast by his umbrella.

Estelle loved to watch the geese and ducks waddling around in groups. During her first few days there, she had been very frightened by the pigs, whose sudden dashes to and fro, their fat bodies wobbling on slender legs, kept her in constant fear of being bumped into and knocked over. Added to that they were filthy, with their mud-blackened bellies and their grubby snouts snuffling at the ground. But Hector had assured her that pigs were earth's best-behaved children, so now their crazy running around at feeding time amused her and she marveled at their pink and silken look when it had been raining, as though they were in their party dresses.

She also watched the geese a lot. From some straw-strewn hole at the end of an alley two companies would emerge, each band keeping to its side. They seemed to greet one another by rubbing their beaks together, then mingled and grubbed together in the vegetable peelings. There was one in particular that used to perch on top of a midden and whose round eye, stiff neck, and air of being nailed to the spot as she puffed out her feathery white breast lent her an air of calm majesty—like an empress with a yellow nose—while she surveyed the others poking about on the ground and giving out their raucous cry. Then all at once the big goose would come down from the rubbish heap with a great trumpeting call and all the other geese followed, with their necks stretched out in the same direction, and they marched off with the waddling step of wounded birds. If a dog came near, their necks curved even more and they hissed at it. Estelle clapped her hands and watched this majestic parade of the two companies marching homeward, like people summoned by pressing business. And yet another distraction was to watch pigs and geese going down to the shore each afternoon for a swim, just like human beings.

When Sunday came around, Estelle decided that she ought to go to church. She never went in Paris, but in the country it was something to do, an excuse to dress up and see a few people. What's more, Hector was there, following the service in a big prayer book with a worn binding, over the top of which he looked steadily at her. His lips were unbending, but there was the hint of a smile in his bright eyes.

When the service was finished, he offered her his arm and walked beside her through the little churchyard. And after evening service, there was something else to see—a procession to the cross at the end of the village. At the head walked a peasant bearing a gold-embroidered purple banner on a red staff. Then followed two lines of women, well spaced out. In the middle came the priests—a *curé,* a *vicaire,* and a private chaplain from a nearby country house. They were all singing at the tops of their voices. Right at the end, following a white banner borne by a plump girl with sunburned arms, came the tail of the faithful, dragging along with a clatter of clogs like a flock of stray sheep. When the procession reached the port, the banners and white headdresses of the women stood out against the deep blue of the sea, and the slow-moving line took on an infinite purity in the sunlight.

Estelle found the graveyard very moving, although usually she shrank from anything sad, and on the first day she shuddered at the sight of the tombs that lay beneath her window. The church overlooked the port and the crosses around it seemed to hold out arms to the vastness of ocean and sky. Sometimes, when the wind rose during the night, the gusts from the sea moaned through the plantation of wooden crosses. But Estelle soon got used to it, because there was a certain pleasing gentleness about the tiny cemetery and it seemed to her that the dead were smiling among the living who existed cheek by jowl with them. Around the graveyard was an elbow-high wall barring the way, there in the middle of Piriac, and nobody thought twice about cocking a leg over the wall and following the tracks through the tall grass. Children went there to play and scampered around over the granite slabs. Cats sprang out from their hiding places among the bushes to chase one another, and often the lovesick yowling of she-cats in heat pierced the air as they waited, fur bristling and long tails flailing the air.

There were luxuriant wild plants, such as giant fennel with yellow flowers like parasols, whose strong scent, after the heat of the day, filled all Piriac with their aniseed smell, wafted from the graves. And what a calm, quiet meadow it was at night, when the cemetery seemed to cast its peace over the sleeping village. Shadows hid the crosses and late strollers sat on the granite seats against the wall, while the waves murmured on the shore and the salty tang of the sea was borne inland on the breeze.

One evening, when the Chabres were walking homeward, Estelle, who was leaning on Hector's arm, said that she would like to cross the graveyard. Monsieur Chabre protested that it was a silly, romantic fancy and went round by the quay. The path was so narrow that Estelle had to let go of Hector's arm and her skirt rustled ahead of him through the long grass. So overpowering was the smell of fennel that the lovesick cats did not dart away but stayed bemused under the bushes. As they passed through the shadow cast by the church, Estelle felt Hector's hand touch her waist. She cried out in alarm.

'How silly!' she said as they emerged from the shadows, 'I thought I was about to be carried off by a ghost.'

Hector laughed and explained it away by saying, 'It was probably just a branch or a sprig of fennel that caught against your skirt.'

They stopped and looked at the crosses around them, moved by the profound calm of death, and then went on their way, uneasy in their minds.

'You were frightened, weren't you? I heard you!' said Monsieur Chabre. 'Well, it serves you right.'

They often enjoyed watching the sardine boats that came in on the high tide. When one sailed into port, Hector alerted the Chabres. When he had seen his sixth sardine boat come in, Monsieur Chabre declared that it was merely the same thing over and over again. Estelle, on the other hand, seemed never to tire of the sight and was more excited each time she went down to the jetty. Sometimes she had to run to get there in time, hopping over the uneven stones and holding up her skirts in one hand so as not to trip over them, and letting them fly out behind her. When they got there, she was out of breath and stood with her hands pressed to her breast and her head thrown back to regain her normal breathing. To Hector she seemed irresistible as she stood there, her hair streaming in the wind and a fearless boyish expression on her face.

When a boat had tied up, the fishermen carried ashore their baskets of sardines that sparkled with glints of silver, blue, pink, sapphire, and pale ruby in the rays of the setting sun. Hector explained again and again what was going on. Each basket contained a thousand sardines and in the morning the selling price of a basket would be fixed according to how good the catch was. The fishermen then divided among them the money from the sale, setting aside one third of the total for the owner of the boat. Then the fish were salted and packed in perforated wooden trays through which the brine could drip away.

But little by little, Estelle and her companion turned away from the subject of sardines. Although they still went there, they no longer noticed what went on. They ran all the way there but dragged their feet on the way back, staring in silence at the sea.

And every time they returned from the port, Monsieur Chabre would inquire, 'I hope there's a good catch of sardines?'

'Oh, yes,' they replied, 'a splendid catch.'

Every Sunday evening there was an open-air ball at Piriac. Hand in hand, the local boys and girls turned and turned about for hours on end, singing the same airs in the same low and strongly accented tone. Their untrained voices, rising in the still twilight, had a certain barbaric appeal.

Estelle sat on the beach with Hector at her feet, listening and daydreaming. The tide came in with the deep caressing sound of a passionate voice as the waves broke on the sand, then fading away and dying as the water fell back with the plaintive murmur of a tamed love. The young woman wished that she were loved in such a way, by a giant who, in her hands, would become a small boy.

'Aren't you getting bored at Piriac, dearest?' Monsieur Chabre sometimes asked her.

'Oh, no, dear, not in the slightest,' Estelle hastened to reply.

There was plenty to distract her in that isolated village. Geese, pigs, sardines, everything took on enormous importance for her. The little graveyard was lively. This quiet life with nobody around but the grocer from Nantes and the deaf lawyer from Guérande seemed more exciting than life at noisy and fashionable seaside resorts. After a couple of weeks, Monsieur Chabre was bored to tears and wanted to go home to Paris, declaring that he was sure his shellfish diet must have done its work by now.

But Estelle protested, saying, 'You haven't eaten enough yet, dear. You still need some more —I know you do.'

IV

One evening Hector told the Chabres: 'There's going to be a very high tide tomorrow. We could go shrimping.'

Estelle seemed delighted at the idea. Of course they must go shrimping, this was something she had looked forward to for a long time. Monsieur Chabre raised all kinds of objections. First of all, one never caught anything; then again, it was much easier to go out and buy some for next to nothing from a local fishwife without getting soaked to the waist and gashing your feet on the rocks. In the end, however, he had to give in to his wife's enthusiasm. Some elaborate preparations were made.

Hector was responsible for finding the nets. Despite his horror and fear of cold water, Monsieur Chabre, once he had let himself in for it, intended to put his heart into shrimping. That morning he had a pair of knee boots dubbed and dressed himself in a light linen suit. His wife could not dissuade him from wearing a bow tie and he knotted it carefully and spread out the ends as if he were off to a wedding. This tie of his was nothing but the protest of a respectable man against the slovenliness of the ocean.

As for Estelle, she merely slipped a loose-fitting blouse over her bathing suit. Hector, too, wore a bathing suit.

The three of them set off at about two o'clock in the afternoon with nets over their shoulders. To reach the rocks where Hector said there were plenty of shrimps, they had to walk about a mile and a half across sand and seaweed. He led the way, walking steadily in a straight line without worrying about pools of water or anything else that lay in his path. Estelle followed him boldly, delighted by the dampness of the shore and splashing gaily with her little feet. Monsieur Chabre, bringing up the rear, saw no necessity for getting his boots wet before even getting to a place where they could fish. He went around each puddle carefully, jumped over the runnels of water in the sand, and picked out the dry spots with that calculating care a Parisian shows when walking down the Rue Vivienne on a muddy day. He got out of breath quickly and kept asking: 'Is it very much farther, Monsier Hector? Look, why don't we try here—I am sure I can see some shrimps. Anyway, they're everywhere in the sea, aren't they? I bet we'd only have to put our nets in the water to get some.'

'All right, Monsieur Chabre, try it,' Hector answered.

This being a good excuse for him to get his breath back, Monsieur Chabre drew his net through a pool of water not much bigger than the palm of his hand. The puddle was completely empty and he didn't even catch a piece of seaweed. So off he went again, wrapped in dignity and pursing his lips. But since he wanted to prove that you could catch shrimps anywhere in the sea, he ended up a good way behind the others.

The tide was still running out and the sea was a good three quarters of a mile from the shore. Drained of water, the rocks and pebbles of the sea bed spread as far as the eye could see in a damp, uneven, and deserted stretch of foreshore that in its desolate grandeur was like a wide, flat land laid waste by a storm. Far off, the sea lay in an ever-retreating green line, as though the earth were drinking it down. The rocks, lying in long bands of black, rose from the water into still headlands. Estelle stood and looked at the great empty space before her and murmured, 'How big it is!'

Hector pointed out to her certain rocks packed like a green floor worn by the swell of the ocean. 'This only becomes visible twice a month,' he said. 'That is where the mussels come from. Can you see that brown mark over there? That's the Red Cows—the best place for lobsters—and they only show above the water at neap tide. But let's hurry. We're going to those rocks over there that are just beginning to show.'

Estelle loved going into the water and lifted her feet and splashed about, laughing aloud at the spray she raised. When she was in up to her knees, she had to fight against the tide. Walking quickly through the water, she loved the sensation of its resistance and the running of the tide against her legs.

'Don't be afraid,' said Hector. 'You'll go in up to your waist, but the water gets shallower after that and we're nearly there.'

And so they were when, having crossed a narrow arm of the sea, they found themselves in shallow water on a sort of platform of rocks left by the tide. When Estelle turned to see which way they had come, she could not help exclaiming aloud. They were such a long way from the shore! Piriac was far off down the coast, nothing but a smudge of white to mark the houses and the square church tower with green shutters rising above them. She had never seen anything like it: the sun beating down on golden sands, dark green seaweed, and the damp and gleaming colors of the rocks. It was like the end of the world, a space filled with ruins at the edge of nothingness.

Estelle and Hector were just about to start fishing when they heard a pathetic cry. Monsieur Chabre was standing in the middle of the creek and wanted to know which way to go. 'How do you get across here?' he shouted. 'Do I go straight ahead? Tell me!'

He was up to his waist in water and dared not venture another step, terrified of walking into a hole and vanishing.

'Go to the left!' Hector shouted at him.

Monsieur Chabre went to the left but, finding he was getting in still deeper, he stopped again without even having the courage to turn and go back. He just stood there and whined.

'Come and give me a hand. I know there are holes here. I can feel them.'

'Go to the right, Monsieur Chabre, to the right!' Hector shouted.

The poor man looked so funny, standing there in the middle of the water with his shrimping net over his shoulder and his elegant bow tie under his chin, that Estelle and Hector could not help laughing. At last he go out of his difficulties, but when he reached the other two, he seemed very shaken and burst out furiously, 'Do you realize that I can't swim?'

Then he began worrying about how to get back, and when Hector explained that he would have to watch out that the tide did not catch him on the rock where he stood, he started fussing again.

'You'll let me know in good time, won't you?'

'Oh, I'll look after you, don't be afraid of that.'

So the three of them started fishing for shimps, trawling their narrow nets through the pools of water. Estelle went at it with all the passion of which a woman is capable—and she caught the first shrimps. Three big ones leaped about in the bottom of her net. They were so big that she was frightened and called Hector over to help her. When she saw that they no longer moved when they were grasped by the head, she got used to it and put them with her own fingers into the little bag slung over her shoulder. Sometimes she raked up a bunch of seaweed and had to pick through it until a tiny scraping sound, like beating wings, told her that she had caught something. She sorted through the seaweed, carefully throwing it away bit by bit, and not completely at ease with those strange bits of vegetation that felt as soft and sticky as dead fish. Every now and then she looked impatiently into her basket to see if it was filling up.

'There's a certain knack to it,' said Monsieur Chabre over and over again. 'I haven't caught a single one.'

Since he dared not go into the gaps between the rocks and was weighed down by his big boots full of water, he dragged his net around on the sand and caught nothing but crabs—sometimes five, eight, or ten at a time. He was terribly frightened by them and had a considerable struggle to get them out of his net. Every now and then he turned around and looked anxiously toward the sea to make sure that the tide was still going out.

'Are you sure it's still going down?' he asked Hector.

Hector merely nodded and went on fishing like someone who knew just where to go. With each sweep he caught a whole bunch of shrimps, and when he took his net out of the water he happened to be near Estelle and put his catch into her basket. She laughed, winking behind her husband's back and putting a finger to her lips. She looked so appealing, leaning on the handle of her net or bending her fair head over it, sparkling with impatience to know what she had caught. There was a slight breeze and the water dripping from her bathing suit spattered into tiny drops that lay on her like dew, and her swimsuit clung close to her body and showed her splendid figure to full advantage.

They fished for almost two hours before stopping for a rest. Estelle was out of breath, her hair damp with sweat, and all around her lay a wide, empty space over which complete peace reigned. Only the sea was moving, undulating and murmuring with its gentle voice. At four o'clock on that sunny afternoon, the sky had become such a pale blue that it was almost gray, but despite this furnace-like glare, the heat was not overpowering and a coolness blew in from the sea to dilute and soften the cruel light. Estelle was intrigued by a group of black dots standing out on the rocks against the horizon. These dots were, like themselves, people fishing for shrimps, and they stood out in sharp outline, no bigger than ants and somewhat ridiculous in the middle of such an enormous emptiness. She could see how they were standing—the bent lines of their backs as they drew their nets through the water, or upright, with arms extended and waving like flies' legs, as they inspected their catch. She could even see them sorting out the crabs and seaweed.

'I'm sure the tide has turned!' exclaimed Monsieur Chabre in an anguished voice. 'Look at that rock over there—a moment ago it was standing right out of the water.'

'Yes, the tide is probably coming in,' Hector was provoked into saying impatiently. 'And that's just the time to catch plenty of shrimps.'

Monsieur Chabre began to lose his head. He had just swept his net through the water and caught a strange fish, a sea devil, and was terrified by the sight of its monstrous head. He had had enough.

'Come on, let's go, let's go!' he kept saying. 'It's absurd to take risks!'

'But Hector just said that you can catch a lot

of shrimps when the tide is coming in,' his wife said.

'Oh, the tide's coming in all right!' Hector added in a low voice, his eyes glinting with mischief.

And, in fact, the waves were getting higher and fretting at the rocks with a louder insistence. Swift inroads were made across a whole tongue of land. The conquering sea was returning, reclaiming foot by foot its domain that it had been sweeping across for centuries. Estelle had found a little pool where long seaweed grew, seaweed as fine as hair, and there she was catching enormous shrimps. She drew a swathe through the water like a reaper and nothing was going to get her away from it.

'Well, I don't care, I'm off!' said Monsieur Chabre, with tears in his voice. 'It's ridiculous, we shall be caught here.'

He set off, desperately plumbing with the handle of his shrimping net the depth of the holes in front of his feet. When he had gone two or three hundred yards Hector persuaded Estelle to follow him.

'The water will come right up to our shoulders,' he said with a smile. 'Monsieur Chabre will get a real ducking. Look how deep he's in already.'

Ever since they had set out, Hector had had the sly, preoccupied expression of a lover who has decided to declare his love but has not plucked up courage to do so. When he put the shrimps he caught into Estelle's basket, he tried to touch her fingers. At the same time, he was annoyed at his own lack of initiative. If Monsieur Chabre got himself drowned, Hector would have been delighted because, for the first time, he found him in the way.

'You know what you ought to do?' he said suddenly. 'You should climb on my back and I'll carry you. Otherwise you're going to get soaked through. What about it? Come on, get up.'

He went down, proffering his back to her. Embarrassed and blushing, she refused, but he bullied her and told her he was responsible for her safety, so she climbed onto his back and grasped his shoulders. He was as solid as a rock and straightened up as though she were no heavier than a bird. He told her to hold on tight and then set off into the water.

'I go to the right here, don't I, Monsieur Hector?' Monsieur Chabre cried piteously, with the water already slapping against the small of his back.

'Yes, keep to the right, to the right! All the way!'

And as Estelle's husband turned his back on them, shivering with fright and feeling the sea rising under his armpits, Hector seized the opportunity to kiss one of the tiny hands gripping his shoulders. Estelle was about to snatch her hand away but he told her not to move, because if she did, he would not hold himself responsible for what happened to them—and he began covering her hands with kisses. Her hands were cool and salty and held the sharp, voluptuous taste of the sea.

'Please! Please let me alone' Estelle kept saying, trying to sound angry. 'You really are taking advantage . . . If you do it again, I shall jump into the water.'

He kept on kissing her hands and she did not jump. He held her ankles tight, he kissed her hands hungrily—all without saying a word, glancing occasionally at Monsieur Chabre's back, that pitifully small portion of back that seemed to sink deeper into the water with every step.

'Did you tell me to go to the right?' Monsieur Chabre implored.

'Go to the left if you want to!'

Monsieur Chabre took a step to the left and yelped. He went in right up to his neck, so deep that even his bow tie was under water. This put Hector completely at ease and he made his declaration.

'I love you, Madame.'

'Shush, Monsieur! I forbid you to speak.'

'I love you, I adore you, and I have kept quiet

until now only out of respect.'

He did not look at her but plodded along through the water, which now came up to his chest. The situation struck Estelle as being so funny that she could not help laughing out loud.

'Oh, look here, do keep quiet,' she said again in a maternal way, slapping him on the shoulder. 'Behave yourself and, above all, don't fall down in the water.'

That slap on the shoulder thrilled Hector to the core. It seemed to set the seal on everything. Noticing Estelle's husband still rooted to the spot in his distress, he called out gaily, 'Go straight ahead!'

When they got to the beach, Monsieur Chabre embarked on a long explanation.

'I swear I nearly got drowned out there,' he spluttered. 'It's these boots I'm wearing.'

Estelle opened her basket and showed it to him, full of shrimps.

'You mean to say you caught all those?' he exclaimed in amazement. 'Well, you certainly know how to fish.'

'Oh,' she said, smiling at Hector, 'Monsieur taught me.'

V

The Chabres had only two more days to spend at Piriac. Hector seemed dismayed, annoyed, and downcast at the same time. Monsieur Chabre, for his part, thought each morning about his health and appeared to be puzzled.

'You simply can't go without having seen the Castelli rocks,' said Hector one evening. 'We must arrange a trip there tomorrow.'

He gave a detailed explanation. The rocks were only a mile away and followed the coast-line in a wide curve pitted with caves and fretted by the sea. It was, he said, the loneliest stretch of coast imaginable.

'All right, let's go tomorrow,' said Estelle when he had finished talking. 'Is it very hard going?'

'No, there are one or two places where you get your feet wet but that's all.'

But Monsieur Chabre had no intention of getting his feet wet again. Ever since the soaking he got when they went shrimping he had felt a grudge against the sea. He was violently opposed to this new trip. Taking risks was stupid, for one thing, and, for another, he had not the slightest intention of jumping around like a mountain goat and breaking a leg. What he would do, if they were absolutely set on going, was to accompany them as far as the top of the cliff—and that was making a great concession.

In order to pacify him, Hector had a sudden inspiration and said: 'I've got an idea. On the way, you have to go past the semaphore at Castelli, so why don't you call in there and buy some shellfish from the telegraph men. They always have some beauties and they almost give them away.'

'That *is* a good idea,' said Monsieur Chabre, in sudden good humour, 'I'll take a small basket with me and have a last good feed of shellfish.'

He turned to his wife and said in what he considered to be a roguish way, 'Who knows? Perhaps this lot will do the trick!'

Next day they had to wait for low tide before setting out. Then Estelle was not ready and it was five o'clock in the afternoon before they left. Hector said that it did not matter and they would not be caught by the tide when it came in. Estelle wore canvas shoes on her bare feet and a very short, gray linen dress that she tucked up so that it showed her slender ankles. Monsieur Chabre, of course, was meticulously dressed in a pair of white trousers and an alpaca jacket. He carried his umbrella and a small basket and looked like a Parisian setting forth on a shopping expedition.

The path to the rocks was difficult and they walked along a beach of shifting sand in which their feet sank. Monsieur Chabre started to pant like an ox. 'Well, I'm going to leave you here. I'll go up to the top,' he puffed.

'That's right,' replied Hector. 'If you take that path there, you can climb up but farther along you won't be able to. Do you want a hand? Quite sure you don't?'

And they watched him until he reached the top of the cliff where he opened his umbrella and, swinging his basket, shouted down to them, 'I'm up! And it's better here! Be careful down there, mind! Anyway, I'll keep an eye on you.'

Hector and Estelle set off between the rocks. The young man led the way and jumped, in his high boots, from stone to stone with the graceful strength of a mountain huntsman. Estelle followed him fearlessly by the same stones and when he turned to her and said, 'Do you want to take my hand?' she replied, 'No, of course not. What do you think I am, an old lady?'

They got to a kind of spreading floor of granite that the sea had worked into deep furrows. Showing through the sand, it seemed like the bones of some monster whose dislocated vertebrae broke through the surface. In the hollows were little channels of water and tresses of black seaweed. The young couple leaped on their way, sometimes balancing on a rock and laughing aloud when it rocked beneath their feet.

'It's just like home here,' said Estelle gaily. 'You could put these rocks in the drawing room!'

'You just wait and see,' said Hector.

They came to a narrow gap, a sort of split yawning between two enormous blocks and there, lying below, was a small pool right in their path.

'I shall never get through there,' said Estelle.

Hector offered to carry her but she refused, slowly shaking her head, because she did not want to be carried by him again. So they looked around for big stones to make a bridge with. But the stones slid into the bottom of the water.

'Give me your hand, I'm going to jump over,' she suddenly said impatiently.

She jumped, but one foot fell short of the other side and went into the water, at which both of them burst out laughing. Then, as they emerged from the narrow passage, a cry of admiration burst from her lips.

Before them was a creek filled with a gigantic avalanche of rocks. Among the waves, enormous blocks of granite stood upright like sentinels. All along the cliffs, storms and rough weather had clawed away at the earth until nothing was left but great, bare masses of granite. Between the spurs of rock were bays and sharp turnings that led into vaultlike hollows, while on the sand slabs of blackish marble lay like great stranded fish. It was a sort of cyclopean city that had been stormed and taken and sacked by the sea, its defenses brought down, its towers half ruined, and its buildings toppled one upon the other.

Hector showed Estelle every nook and cranny of these ruins wrought by the sea. She walked on sand as fine and golden as powdered gold, on pebbles streaked with mica that sparkled in the sun, over tumbled rocks where she had to use both hands in order not to fall into the holes between them. She passed through doorways of rock, under triumphal arches rounded in Roman style or soaring upward to a Gothic point. She went down into cool hollows, into deserts measuring no more than ten square yards. She glanced smilingly at the mauve sea thistles and dark green grass staining the gray walls of the cliffs and watched the small brown sea birds flying shoulder high and continuously uttering their faint twittering cries. What surprised her most of all was to turn from the rocks and find the sea always there, the blue line of its majestic calm constantly reappearing and changing in length according to the gaps between the rocks through which it was glimpsed.

'Ah, there you are!' Monsieur Chabre shouted from the top of the cliff. 'I was getting worried because you were completely out of sight. I say! Those gaps in the rocks are terrifying, aren't they?'

He was standing, with extreme caution, at least six feet from the edge of the cliff, umbrella held in one hand over his head and his basket hooked over his other arm.

'The tide's coming in very fast so you'd better watch out,' he added.

'Don't worry, we've got plenty of time,' Hector replied.

Estelle, sitting on a rock and looking out at the wide horizon, said nothing. Before her stood three granite pillars worn smooth by the waves, like great columns of a ruined temple. Behind them the rising sea stretched away, royal blue and streaked gold in the light of the evening sun. Between two of the pillars she could see a distant sail, as blindingly white as a gull's wing sweeping the water. The pale sky was already filled with the calm of twilight and Estelle had never before known such a deep and tender feeling.

'Come along,' said Hector, touching her hand.

She shivered and stood up, abandoning herself to the feeling of languor that possessed her.

'Is that the semaphore over there, the little building with the mast?' Monsieur Chabre called down to them. 'I'll go and get some shellfish and catch up with you later.'

Estelle started to run like a child, trying to shake off her listlessness. She leaped over pools of water and made toward the sea in a sudden determination to clamber over a jumble of rocks that the incoming tide was about to transform into an island. After an upward struggle through the gaps in the rocks, she reached the summit and hauled herself onto the highest rock of all and stood there, exhilarated, high above the dramatic desolation of the coastline. Her delicate profile stood out against the clear air and her skirt fluttered like a flag in the wind.

On the way down, she leaned over and peered into all the gaping holes between the rocks. In each small crevice were tiny, calm, limpid pools in which the sky was reflected. At the bottom lay romantic forests of emerald seaweed. Nothing moved there but the great black crabs scuttling and vanishing as quickly as frogs without even disturbing the surface of the water. Estelle watched, plunged into a dream, as if mysterious landscapes and countries, full of unknown wonders, were revealed to her.

When they got back to the foot of the cliffs, she noticed that Hector was carrying a handkerchief filled with winkles.

'These are for Monsieur Chabre,' he said. 'I'll take them up to him.'

Just at that moment, Monsieur Chabre came into view again and gave a loud cry of disappointment. 'There's not a single mussel in the semaphore hut! I never wanted to come in the first place and it turned out that I was absolutely right!'

When the young man held up the winkles, Monsieur Chabre calmed down and he was dumfounded by Hector's agility in climbing the cliff by a path that only he knew and that seemed to go up a rock face as smooth as a well. The descent seemed even more spectacular.

'There's nothing to it,' said Hector. 'It's just like a stairway—you just have to know where the steps are.'

Monsieur Chabre was alarmed by the rising tide and wanted to go home. He begged his wife at least to climb up by an easy path. Hector laughed and replied that there were no paths suitable for ladies and that they would both have to stick it out to the end. Furthermore, they had not visited the caves. So Monsieur Chabre had to resign himself to setting off alone along the cliff top. As the sun was setting, he used his umbrella as a walking stick and carried his basket of winkles in the other hand.

'Are you tired?' Hector asked gently.

'Yes, a little,' Estelle replied.

She took his arm and, although she did not feel tired in the least, a delightful sensation of abandon filled her from one moment to the next. She still trembled inside from the excitement she had felt as she watched Hector swarming up the side of the cliff. They walked slowly across a strip of beach and the broken shells crunched under their feet like the gravel in a garden path. They no longer spoke a word. He showed her two large fissures, the Mad Monk's Cave and the Cat's Grotto. She went in and looked around with no more reaction than a tiny shiver. When they started walking again along a stretch of sandy strand, they looked at each other with a silent smile. The sea was coming in in short whispering waves and they no longer heard it. Above them, Monsieur Chabre started shouting and they did not hear him either.

'What madness!' the retired grain merchant said over and over again, waving his unbrella and his basket of winkles. 'Estelle! Monsieur Hector! You'll be caught by the tide! It's up to your feet already.'

But they did not even notice the cool lapping of the waves.

'What? What's the matter?' whispered Estelle at last.

'Oh, it's you, Monsieur Chabre,' said Hector. 'Don't worry, nothing's wrong. There's nothing left to see but the Lady's Grotto.'

Monsieur shrugged in despair and replied, 'It's sheer madness! You'll get drowned!'

But they were no longer listening to him, and to escape from the rising crosstides they passed from rock to rock and came at last to the Lady's Grotto, a cave hollowed out of a block of granite jutting out into the sea. The high ceiling was rounded out to form a great dome and the walls had been worn to a gleaming agate-like smoothness by the stormy seas. Veins of pink and blue whirled in barbaric arabesques in the dark rock, as if primitive artists had decorated the cave as a bathroom for the queens of the sea. The gravel of the floor, still damp, held a transparent gleam, like a bed of precious stones. At the back of the cave was a bank of soft, dry sand that was so pale as to be almost white.

Estelle sat on the sand and looked around the cave.

'It's a place you could live in,' she murmured.

Hector appeared to look out toward the sea for a moment and suddenly pretended to be dismayed.

'My God, we're caught! The tide has cut us off and we shall have to wait here for a couple of hours.'

This information annoyed Monsieur Chabre. So they would miss their dinner? Speaking for himself, he was already hungry. This was a funny kind of outing! Grumbling, he sat down on the short grass, umbrella to the left of him and basket of winkles to the right.

'All right, then, I'll wait since I have no choice!' he shouted back. 'See that my wife doesn't catch cold.'

Hector sat beside Estelle in the cave and after a a moment of silence he ventured to take her hand. She made no attempt to withdraw it and sat looking into the distance to where the night was falling and a dusting of cloud darkened the setting sun little by little. On the horizon the sky took on a faint violet shade, slowly darkening and without a sail in sight. Gradually the sea entered the cave, to roll with a whispering sound the transparent pebbles, bringing with it the voluptuousness of the deep, a caressing sound and a tang sharp with longing.

'I love you, Estelle,' Hector said again and again, covering her hands with kisses.

She did not reply, as though she were stifled and carried beyond herself by the rising sea. She was now half lying on the fine sand, like a water nymph taken by surprise and defenseless.

Suddenly Monsieur Chabre's voice, faint and disembodied, reached their ears.

'Aren't you hungry down there? I'm famished! It's just as well that I've got my knife with me so that I can have a snack of winkles!'

'I love you, Estelle,' repeated Hector, holding her in his arms.

It was dark now and the whiteness of the ocean was reflected in the sky. At the mouth of the cave, the sea moaned and the last glimmer of daylight faded beneath the vaulted dome. A smell of fertility was carried in by the rolling waves and Estelle laid her head on Hector's shoulder. Sighs were borne away on the evening breeze.

On his cliff top, Monsieur Chabre chewed his way methodically through his winkles by the light of the stars. Having no bread, he gorged himself to the point of indigestion.

VI

Nine months after her return to Paris, the beautiful Madame Chabre gave birth to a boy. Monsieur Chabre was beside himself with joy. Taking aside Dr. Guiraud, he confided proudly, 'I'll bet you anything you like it was the winkles that did it. One evening I ate a whole basket of winkles under somewhat peculiar circumstances —but that's neither here nor there. Frankly Doctor, I had no idea that shellfish were so beneficial in that respect.'

Sphere Books include:

SPHERE STOCKLIST arranged by subject: authors are alphabetically arranged within subject category.

BIOGRAPHY AND AUTOBIOGRAPHY

Duke of Bedford	A Silver-Plated Spoon	5/–
Cordelia Drexel Biddle	The Happiest Millionaire	5/–
Henry Blyth	The Pocket Venus	7/6
Winston S. Churchill	Marlborough—Volume 1 (illus. with maps)	12/6
Winston S. Churchill	Marlborough—Volume 2 (illus. with maps)	12/6
Winston S. Churchill	Marlborough—Volume 3 (illus. with maps)	12/6
Winston S. Churchill	Marlborough—Volume 4 (illus. with maps)	12/6
Winston S. Churchill	Marlborough—Volumes 1, 2, 3 & 4 (illus. with maps) presentation case	50/–
Maurice Hennessy	I'll Come Back in the Springtime (illus.)	5/–
Margery Hurst	No Glass Slipper	5/–
Doris Lessing	In Pursuit of the English	5/–
Lord Moran	Winston Churchill: The Struggle for Survival 1940/1965	9/6
Sean O'Faolain	Constance Markievicz	6/–
Oliver St. John Gogarty	As I was Going Down Sackville Street	7/6
Peter Scott	Happy the Man (illus. together with a decorative screen of a specially commissioned full-colour Peter Scott painting in a presentation case)	15/–

DOMESTIC SCIENCE

Robert Carrier	Great Dishes of the World	10/6
Robert Carrier	The Robert Carrier Cookbook	19/6
Robert Carrier	Great Dishes of the World & The Robert Carrier Cookbook	30/–

GENERAL FICTION

Marcel Ayme	The Conscience of Love	4/–
H. E. Bates	Spella Ho	5/–
Vicki Baum	Flight of Fate	5/–
Vicki Baum	The Weeping Wood	7/6
Walter Baxter	Look Down in Mercy	5/–
Michael J. Bird	Bedazzled	3/6
Heinrich Böll	The Train was on Time	3/6
Elizabeth Bowen	The House in Paris	4/–
John Buchan	The Runagates Club	5/–
Erskine Caldwell	Love and Money	5/–
Henry Cecil	Fathers in Law	5/–
Henry Cecil	Portrait of a Judge	5/–
Alfred Chester	Behold Goliath	7/6
Alfred Chester	Jamie is my Heart's Desire	5/–
James Clavell	Tai-Pan	10/6
Winston Clewes	The Violent Friends	5/–
Robert Donaldson & Michael Joseph	Cane!	5/–

John Dos Passos	Three Soldiers	7/6
Elaine Dundy	The Old Man And Me	5/–
Jane Gaskell	Atlan	5/–
Jane Gaskell	The City	5/–
Jane Gaskell	The Serpent	5/–
Frank Hardy	Power Without Glory	12/6
John Hawkes	Second Skin	6/–
Raynor Heppenstall	The Blaze of Noon	4/–
Chester Himes	If He Hollers Let Him Go	5/–
John Clellon Holmes	The Horn	3/6
Christopher Isherwood	All the Conspirators	3/6
Larry Kenyon	Don Miles: Challenge at le Mans	5/–
Doris Lessing	Retreat to Innocence	5/–
Sinclair Lewis	Dodsworth	6/–
Thomas Mann	Joseph and His Brothers—4 volumes together in a slipcase	42/–
Thomas Mann	Volume I The Tales of Jacob	10/6
Thomas Mann	Volume II Young Joseph	10/6
Thomas Mann	Volume III Joseph In Egypt	10/6
Thomas Mann	Volume IV Joseph The Provider	10/6
Van Wyck Mason	Trouble in Burma	3/6
Hugh Mills	Prudence and the Pill	5/–
Yukio Mishima	Confessions of a Mask	4/–
Nancy Mitford	Love in a Cold Climate	5/–
Erich Maria Remarque	Three Comrades	7/6
Robert H. Rimmer	That Girl From Boston	3/6
Irwin Shaw	Tip on a Dead Jockey	5/–
Irwin Shaw	The Troubled Air	7/6
Wilfred Sheed	A Middle Class Education	7/6
Manning Lee Stokes	Grand Prix	3/6
Irving Stone	Sailor on Horseback	6/–
Jerrard Tickell	Appointment with Venus	3/6
Tereska Torres	Women's Barracks	5/–
B. Traven	The Death Ship	6/–
Henry Treece	The Green Man	5/–
William Trevor	A Standard of Behaviour	3/6
Rex Warner	The Aerodrome	7/6
Herman Wouk	Aurora Dawn	5/–

HISTORY

Joel Carmichael	A Short History of the Russian Revolution	5/–
Leon Trotsky	History of the Russian Revolution Volume 1	10/–
Leon Trotsky	History of the Russian Revolution Volume 2	10/–
Leon Trotsky	History of the Russian Revolution Volume 3	10/–
Leon Trotsky	History of the Russian Revolution— Volumes 1, 2 & 3, Presentation case	30/–

HUMOUR

Patrick Campbell	All Ways on Sundays	5/–
Ingrams & Wells	Mrs. Wilson's Diaries	5/–
James Thurber	Thurber Country	5/–
Anonymous	Why Was He Born So Beautiful & Other Rugby Songs	5/–

SPHERE BOOKS LIMITED—SOLE AGENTS

AFRICA—Kenya, Uganda, Tanzania, Zambia, Malawi: Thomas Nelson & Sons
    Ltd., Kenya
    South Africa, Rhodesia: Thomas Nelson & Sons (Africa) (Pty) Ltd.,
      Johannesburg
    Ghana, Nigeria, Sierra Leone: Thomas Nelson & Sons Ltd., Nigeria
    Liberia: Wadih M. Captan
    Angola, Mozambique: Electroliber Limitada, Angola
    Zambia: Kingstons (North) Ltd.
    Ethiopia: G. P. Giannopoulos
AUSTRALIA—Thomas Nelson (Australia) Ltd.
AUSTRIA—Danubia-Auslieferung
BAHAMAS—Calypso Distributors Ltd.
BELGIUM—Agence et Messageries del la Presse, S.A.
BERMUDA—Baxter's Bookshop Ltd.
CANADA—Thomas Nelson & Sons (Canada) Ltd.
CARIBBEAN—Roland I. Khan (Trinidad)
DENMARK—Danske Boghandleres Bogimport a/s
FRANCE—Librairie Etrangere, Hachette
GERMANY—Distropa Buchvertrieb
GIBRALTAR—Estogans Agencies Ltd.
GREECE—Hellenic Distribution Agency Ltd.
HOLLAND—Van Ditmar
HONG KONG—Western Publications Distribution Agency (H.K.) Ltd.
IRAN—I.A.D.A.
IRAQ—Dar Alaruba Universal Distribution Co.
ISRAEL—Steimatzky's Agency Ltd.
ITALY—Agenzia Internazionale di Distribuzione
KUWAIT—Farajalla Press Agency
LEBANON—The Levant Distributors Co.
LUXEMBOURG—Distropa Buchvertrieb
MALAYSIA, SINGAPORE and BRUNEI—Marican & Sons (Malaysia)
    (Sdn) Berhad
MALTA—Progress Press Co. Ltd.
MIDDLE EAST—Ajamian Brothers, International Publishers Representatives
NEW ZEALAND—Hodder & Stoughton Ltd.
PORTUGAL—Electroliber Limitada
SOUTH AMERICA—Colombia: Liberia Central
    Chile: Libreria Studio
    Mexico and Central America: Libreria Britanica
    Peru: Librerias ABC
    Venezuela: Distribuidora Santiago
SPAIN—Commercial Atheneum
SUDAN—Sudan Bookshop
SWEDEN—Importbokhandeln
SWITZERLAND—Friedr. Daeniker
THAILAND—The Pramuansarn Publishing House
TURKEY—Librairie Hachette